A Sydney Ce

Welcome to Sydne

Harper, Ivy, Alinta and Phoebe have reached the top at Sydney Central. Along the way, they've weathered the highs and lows of life, but one thing has always remained steadfast: their friendship!

Now life's about to take an unexpected turn for the friends—it seems that Cupid has checked in to Sydney Central Hospital!

Come and experience the rush of falling in love as these four feisty heroines meet their matches...

Harper and the Single Dad by Amy Andrews

Ivy's Fling with the Surgeon by Louisa George

Ali and the Rebel Doc by Emily Forbes

Phoebe's Baby Bombshell by JC Harroway

All available now!

Dear Reader,

I hope you enjoy reading *Phoebe's Baby Bombshell*. Writing this heartwarming story set within the emotionally charged world of neonatal surgery was great fun, especially given the strong female friendships at the center of this series set in Sydney Central Hospital. Exploring Phoebe and Zach's relationship journey against the backdrop of their chosen medical field while they shared the secret of their own baby added another layer to the emotional dynamic this couple faced in search of their happy ending.

Happy reading!

Love,

JC xx

PHOEBE'S BABY BOMBSHELL

———

JC HARROWAY

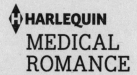

HARLEQUIN

MEDICAL
ROMANCE

Special thanks and acknowledgment are given to JC Harroway for her contribution to A Sydney Central Reunion miniseries.

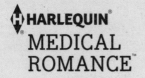

HARLEQUIN®
MEDICAL
ROMANCE™

Recycling programs
for this product may
not exist in your area.

ISBN-13: 978-1-335-59487-7

Phoebe's Baby Bombshell

Copyright © 2023 by Harlequin Enterprises ULC

For questions and comments about the quality of this book, please contact us at CustomerService@Harlequin.com.

Harlequin Enterprises ULC
22 Adelaide St. West, 41st Floor
Toronto, Ontario M5H 4E3, Canada
www.Harlequin.com

Printed in U.S.A.

Lifelong romance addict **JC Harroway** took a break from her career as a junior doctor to raise a family and found her calling as a Harlequin author instead. She now lives in New Zealand and finds that writing feeds her very real obsession with happy endings and the endorphin rush they create. You can follow her at jcharroway.com and on Facebook, Twitter and Instagram.

Books by JC Harroway

Harlequin Medical Romance

Gulf Harbour ER

Tempted by the Rebel Surgeon
Breaking the Single Mom's Rules

Forbidden Fling with Dr. Right
How to Resist the Single Dad

Harlequin DARE

The Proposition
Bad Business
Bad Reputation
Bad Mistake
Bound to You
Tempting the Enemy

Visit the Author Profile page
at Harlequin.com for more titles.

To female friendships and the laughter,
tears and joy they inspire.

**Praise for
JC Harroway**

"Temptation at its very best! JC Harroway delights
her readers with a forbidden romance and it does
not disappoint! I highly recommend this book to
anyone who loves a clandestine romance with lots
of sparks and so much heart."

—*Goodreads* on *Bound to You*

PROLOGUE

DR PHOEBE MASON maintained her composed smile as her colleague, world-renowned neonatal surgeon Zachary Archer, respectfully contradicted her opinion, flashing her the mildly apologetic version of his confident smile before giving his answer to the member of the audience.

Phoebe shivered, gripping the microphone tighter, both flattered by his flirty look and niggled that he'd failed to agree with her suggested management of patent ductus arteriosus, or PDA.

Of course she could handle his professional challenge. As Head of Neonatal Surgery at Sydney Central Hospital, she was usually considered the expert at the Advances in Neonatal Surgery conference, which this year was being held in Brisbane. But with the presence of Dr Archer, a man known for his unfailing self-belief, ambition and that intuitive edge that some people deemed arrogance, the questions posed to the panel of experts on the stage had never been more vigorously debated.

'…and while the recommended intervention for pre-term neonates of this age and weight is open heart surgery,' Zachary Archer said, glancing pointedly at Phoebe once more so a titter of nervous laughter passed around the auditorium, 'I have had success with cardiac catheterisation in patients weighing as little as seven hundred grams.'

Catching the spark of rivalry in his gunmetal-grey eyes, Phoebe looked away, fighting the urge to say something…provocative. While they had attended conferences together before, they'd never actually met. But there had always been something about Zach Archer that called to the woman in her, a woman who had little time and even less inclination for the demands of a personal life. Except something about the way he'd looked at her with amusement twitching his lips and interest in his eyes made her raise the microphone to address the audience once more.

'Of course,' she said, 'while a trans-catheter closure of PDA is minimally invasive and therefore preferable in terms of operative risk reduction and shortened recovery time for the patient, I think we can all agree that, with the exception of my esteemed colleague Dr Archer, for the more… cautious surgeon, open heart surgery is considered standard for very low birth weight patients.'

'Next question,' the panel facilitator stated,

carrying the microphone to another audience member with their hand raised.

Aware of her heart thundering with excitement, Phoebe kept her gaze averted from Zachary and stifled her smile. Even so, she sensed his observation, felt it slither over her skin like a wisp of silk. If they were alone and not seated on a stage watched by three hundred delegates, they would definitely be flirting.

What was wrong with her? She hardly ever flirted.

Perhaps it was because today was her fortieth birthday. Perhaps because it was the final day of the conference. Tomorrow she'd return to Sydney, to her jam-packed week at work. Her friends were determined to organise a celebratory night on the town for the milestone, but coordinating everyone's schedules was an impossible task. But it seemed her neglected femininity, not happy to be short-changed, had had enough of work and had staged a revolt, raised an army of hormones targeted at the most single man in the room. Zach Archer was also a notorious commitment-shy bachelor, married to his job, which included high-profile charity work for global neonatal charity Nurture, for which he was often in the media.

Phoebe took some long, slow breaths, dismissing the unexpectedly fierce flare of attraction. The arrival of the big four zero had never bothered her before. She was happy with her career, had all the social contact she required with her mum and her wonderful friends Ali, Harper and Ivy, fellow doctors at Sydney Central Hospital. She'd even recently taken up yoga.

Life was good.

The discussion topic switched to the treatment of Tetralogy of Fallot, and Phoebe passed the microphone to the woman seated to her left, smoothing her palm down her thigh, straightening the wrinkle in her charcoal skirt.

As the conversation once more highlighted the contrast between her surgical approach and that of Dr Archer, she couldn't help but wonder if the sparks demonstrated in their professional differences of opinion would transfer to the bedroom…

Later that evening, at the close of conference social event in the hotel bar, Phoebe sipped her boozy cocktail, the Hanky Panky, for which the cocktail lounge was renowned. Set on the ground floor of the hotel, the dimly lit and luxuriously decorated bar was chic and sophisticated. Floor-to-ceiling sliding doors opened onto the street outside allowing in the warm sultry air and sounds of the vibrant city.

As her conversation with a professor at Sydney's University Hospital—a man with the bushiest grey eyebrows Phoebe had ever seen—came to an end, she found her gaze wandering the gathering, seeking out Zachary Archer. A little light flirtation with someone her own age, someone unmarried and, like her, uninterested in a relationship, might be just the birthday celebration she needed.

She took another gulp of the cocktail, the sinking feeling in her stomach telling her that her sexy colleague had probably already left Brisbane. He grew up in Sydney, but rarely spent any time there. Instead, he travelled the world, consulting on complex cases and performing surgeries that would make other specialists quake in their theatre shoes.

Her degree of dejection forced her to recall the last time she'd been on a date. Was it that guy Ali had set her up with? Some cousin of Ali's cousin whose divorce had just been finalised…? Struggling to picture the man who had been so dull that, by the end of the evening, Phoebe had resented that she had shaved her legs and dressed up, she resigned herself to finishing her Hanky-Panky and heading upstairs to her hotel room to pack her weekend bag.

'Dr Mason.' Over her shoulder a deep voice drawled, sending thrilling little shivers down Phoebe's spine.

She knew that voice, had struggled to erase it from her head since they'd clashed on the dis-

cussion panel that afternoon. Spinning, she faced
Zachary, matching his confident smile with one
of her own.

'Dr Archer,' she said, her voice emerging calm
and unruffled while her stomach took a pleasur-
able tumble. He wore dark jeans and a claret-
coloured slim-fit shirt that made the gold flecks
in his eyes pop and outlined his broad chest and
ripped physique.

'You can call me Zach.' He held out his hand
and Phoebe took it, steeling herself against the
physical contact.

'Phoebe,' she said, sliding her hand from his
warm and firm grip.

Why was his brand of confidence, intuition
and work discipline so attractive? Or was it just
that as a single, self-confessed workaholic he rep-
resented the ultimate in unattainable men and
therefore was a perfectly suited partner for some
harmless flirtatious banter?

You don't need a man, darling.

Her mother's often recited mantra played in her
head as she willed her pulse to calm down after
that handshake. It was true, she didn't, but she
could want one every now and then, especially
when they were as tempting as Zach.

'So you disagree with my methods?' he said
in his direct way, diving straight back into their
earlier debate on their surgical interventions of

choice. The intense stare was back too, a hint of playfulness and a whole lot of interest.

'Only the risky ones.' One of the reasons Phoebe loved her job taking care of tiny, vulnerable babies was because it tapped into the protective aspects of her personality, ones that developed from a childhood of being close to her single-parent mother after being abandoned by her father.

'Are you offended? Is your ego horribly bruised?' Phoebe smiled up at him—even with her wearing heels, he was still taller—her eyes batting as if of their own accord, no doubt fuelled by the gin in her cocktail.

Zach's smile widened, the white of his teeth flashing in the dim lighting. 'It takes a lot more than a little friendly professional debate to damage my ego, I assure you.'

'That's good.' Laughing, Phoebe sipped her lethally strong drink. 'We couldn't have your reputation tarnished by a little healthy competition, now, could we?' Aware she'd slipped seamlessly into full-on flirting mode, Phoebe resolved to sound less breathless the next time she spoke. If he wanted her, she wasn't going to do the grunt work for him.

'I'm not sure which of my reputations you're referring to,' he said conspiratorially, dipping his head closer and dropping his deep voice, 'but I am always open to friendly rivalry, although you should know that I always win. Ask my three siblings.'

His broad smile and cool grey eyes were full of playfulness.

Phoebe laughed again, enjoying herself. 'Where's the fun in that?' As if of their own accord, her feet inched her into his personal space until she was bathed in the heat radiating from his body. She rarely let her hair down, and while her professional success was ultimately fulfilling, she was still a red-blooded woman who deserved to celebrate her birthday. Sparring with him certainly beat packing her bag and an early night.

'The fun is in being the best.' He stepped closer, raised his glass—a high-ball full of ice and amber liquid—to hers and they clinked them together, his stare dipping to her mouth when she took another hasty swallow to conceal her body's eager reaction.

Phoebe rolled her eyes at his arrogance. He didn't need any encouragement. His drive and determination reigned supreme. He knew what he wanted and made it happen.

Did he want her?

'Don't get ahead of yourself, Zach,' she said, her breathing tight. 'You might convince me that you're overcompensating.'

As if answering her unvoiced question, he shot

her a look of pure, unadulterated heat, bending
forward to breathe his reply close to her ear.
'Trust me, I'm the best in all areas of my life.'

The tickle of his breath down her neck made
Phoebe's head spin with longing.

He straightened, held her gaze, stared through
the suspenseful few seconds that passed and then
took a lazy sip from his glass.

Left in no doubt of his interest, Phoebe swallowed hard. 'Well, cheers to that,' she said, her
voice a little croaky.

'Can I get you another drink?' he asked, seeing that she was almost done with her cocktail.

'Perhaps.' Although she was tipsy after one. 'It
is my birthday today, the big four zero.'

He raised his eyebrows in surprise. 'Well, then,
happy birthday, Phoebe.' He spoke her name in
his low and seductive voice, his stare tracing her
features and landing back on her mouth.

It was highly distracting. All she could think
about was what it would feel like to kiss him.
Was she seriously contemplating taking this to
the next level?

As they gazed at each other, non-verbal communication passing between them, the rest of the
bar's patrons seemed to disappear. 'So, are you
leaving Brisbane tomorrow?'

That wasn't too obvious a question. And unless she sensed that, like her, Zach was only in-

terested in commitment-free sex—a one-off, no strings—she would back off.

He nodded. 'I'm off to the UK tomorrow. I have a three-month visiting-surgeon post at London Children's Hospital.' To stop her being jostled by a man carrying four drinks through the throng, Zach took her elbow and guided her closer.

He smelled divine, his expensive-smelling aftershave tickling her nose. Trying not to swoon, Phoebe widened her eyes at his news, impressed. The fact that he was leaving Australia tomorrow solidified her thoughts. Their respective departures in the morning provided a neat end to what could be a perfect night. A gift to herself.

'Well,' she said, draining the last of her drink, her stare drawn to the open neck of his shirt and the tantalising peek of his chest, 'I'll decline that offer of a drink, thanks. These cocktails are lethal and you should probably get some sleep before your early flight. That long haul to London is punishing.'

Reading her subtext, he dipped his excited gaze to her mouth, where she licked the last of the sweet cocktail from her lips. 'I probably should.'

She held out her hand, holding his eye contact as her pulse tripped wildly. 'I'm glad we finally had the opportunity to meet. The debate was… stimulating.'

'I'm glad I could oblige and look forward to our next discussion.' Zach took her hand, this time lingering, his warm grip electrifying the nerves of her arm.

To an observer, they would appear as professional colleagues, shaking hands, the delicious tendrils of sexual chemistry ensnaring them invisible.

'Although, sometimes,' she said, practically whispering now, so turned on by the white-hot smoulder in his stare, she needed to get away from him before the entire bar noticed, 'actions speak louder than words.' Reluctantly releasing his hand, she took one of her hotel-room key cards from her pocket and discreetly pressed it into his hand, her intention loud and clear.

His pupils dilated, his jaw muscles bunching as if he was as desperate to conceal his desires as Phoebe as their fingers brushed. He gripped the card, gripped her hand, holding her captive for a few suspended seconds.

'You're sure?' he asked, his voice low in the crowded and noisy bar.

She nodded, excitement bubbling up in her chest. This thing between them had been brewing all day. They clearly wanted the same thing. 'Absolutely. Room six-three-nine. One night.'

'I can work with that,' he agreed.

They might differ in their professional approaches, her independence and his competitive streak meant they would likely disagree on most things, but when it came to pleasure, they obviously spoke the same language.

Slipping her hand from his, Phoebe left the bar on shaky legs and headed towards the hotel lifts, certain that, after a discreet amount of time, he would follow.

She entered the lift and smiled at her reflection in the mirrored interior whispering *'Happy birthday...'* under her breath.

CHAPTER ONE

Three months later

REACHING THE FRONT of the queue at Perc Up, the café closest to Sydney Central Hospital, and therefore responsible for caffeinating most of the hospital staff, Phoebe swallowed the swell of nausea turning her stomach.

'Can you get me a peppermint tea, please?' she said to a startled Ali at her side, shoving some money at her friend and leaving the line, hurrying away from the normally soothing smell of roasted arabica beans.

Trying to hold onto the half of her breakfast that she'd managed to eat, Phoebe joined Ivy and Harper at a table they'd snagged in the sunny window, which was lush with overhanging plants in pots suspended from industrial-style exposed beams overhead.

As Phoebe took a seat, neither woman paid her much attention. Fortunately they were too caught up in the fact that they were both recently engaged to notice that Phoebe was a little green around the gills.

Zoning out of their chat about wedding guest lists, Phoebe contemplated her situation for what felt like the millionth time. When she'd hooked up with Zach in Brisbane three months ago, she'd hoped for a no-strings night of passion, a gift to herself in celebration of a milestone birthday. What she hadn't anticipated was a condom malfunction and that, at the ripe old age of forty, she'd end up pregnant. The shock of her discovery a few weeks ago was still fresh, compounded by the humiliation that, medically, she would be considered a geriatric mother and the relentless morning sickness she was still trying to hide from her friends and work colleagues.

As Ali joined them at their table, Phoebe plastered a smile on her face and tuned into Ivy and Harper's conversation, which, as it had since Ivy had announced her engagement to her sexy surgeon fiancé, Lucas Matthews, centred on her impending nuptials in seven weeks' time.

'The bridal bouquet is a very serious matter, ladies,' Ivy said, her green eyes bright with excitement and a hint of reprimand that her three maids of honour might indeed take flower choice a little more seriously. 'I need your advice—gardenias or lilies?'

'Definitely lilies—gloriosa are my favourite,'

Phoebe said, throwing herself into the debate to stave off another wave of nausea. She should have declined the invitation to meet this morning before their respective days began, but she hadn't wanted to draw suspicion by her absence and they often gathered at Perc Up for an early pre-work coffee.

A server appeared with Phoebe's tea, attracting curious stares from Ivy and Harper, who were fully aware of Phoebe's usual coffee addiction.

'I have a bit of a headache and a big day in Theatre today,' Phoebe explained, sheepishly glancing down at her pretty teacup and saucer with an internal wince. She hated keeping secrets from her friends.

As if to distract the others from Phoebe's unusual choice of beverage, Ali chipped in, 'Gardenias, definitely gardenias.'

The debate raged on with Harper suggesting lily of the valley.

Phoebe met Ali's sympathetic look with one she hoped conveyed her gratitude. As Head of Obstetrics and Gynaecology at the Central, Ali was the only other person who knew about the pregnancy. Phoebe had never had a regular cycle, so she didn't connect the dots that her one passionate night with Zach had resulted in an unexpected pregnancy until she began to feel nauseous and had developed sore breasts. Then, aware of the risks being an older mother posed, but not ready to confide in anyone, she'd initially consulted Ali for advice on the pretext of 'asking for a friend'. Of course she hadn't been able to fool Ali for ever, eventually coming clean a few days ago.

The coffees arrived and Phoebe shamelessly distracted her friends with more wedding talk. 'What are your favourite flowers, Ivy?'

As her friend gushed excitedly about the amazing florist she'd found to make her bridal bouquet, guilt crept over Phoebe's skin like heat rash.

She wanted to tell Harper and Ivy her news, but she hadn't even told her mother yet. She'd vowed not to tell anyone else until she'd informed Zach.

Her poor, overactive stomach pinched with nerves now that she'd invited thoughts of Zach into her head. While the other three women sipped reviving coffee and chatted animatedly about ceremonies and caterers and honeymoons, Phoebe toyed with her tea, idly swirling the teaspoon around and around for no reason, the pale golden liquid now as unappealing as the idea of coffee.

She would see Zach later that afternoon for the first time since that incredible, but fateful night.

Just over three months ago, she had awoken in her Brisbane hotel room the morning after to find Zach gone. He'd left a brief note, the perfect goodbye, written on a sheet of hotel stationery in his neat, confident handwriting:

I enjoyed helping you to celebrate your birthday.

Take care, Z

And she'd successfully put the wonderful memories behind her, focused on work, which, as for Ali, Harper and Ivy, had included the high-profile case of Emma Wilson, wife of a local celebrity and host of the TV show *If You Build It*, Aaron Wilson, and their twin daughters. Emma was injured in a house fire while still pregnant and was first seen by Harper in the ER before being transferred to Ivy and her fiancé, Lucas, for surgical care. Then, a month ago, Ali delivered Emma's twin girls, Jasmine and Poppy, when she went into premature labour. Now Poppy, who'd been diagnosed with a congenital heart defect, was under Phoebe's care on the neonatal intensive care unit.

But she couldn't put off seeing Zach any longer.

'—and I saw the perfect dresses for you all to wear as my maids of honour,' Ivy said, snagging Phoebe's attention away from her well-versed speech.

Hi, Zach, remember that amazing night in Brisbane? Well...surprise—I'm having your baby!

Latching onto the subject of maid-of-honour dresses instead of indulging her panic, Phoebe tried to smile. Her face felt rubbery, fake. At fourteen weeks pregnant, her favourite trouser suit had been a little tight around the waist that morning. She'd definitely be showing a baby bump by the time Ivy walked down the aisle. There'd be no hiding it in the type of gown Ivy would likely choose for them to wear.

Her time for keeping her secret to herself was running out.

'So, today's the day, huh?' Ivy asked Phoebe, changing the subject so abruptly, Phoebe realised that she must have appeared distracted.

Phoebe stared blankly. All she could think of was that today was the day she would have to tell Zach he was going to be a father.

Frowning, Ivy clarified. 'That guy is arriving, isn't he? The one you've invited to corroborate on, you know, the case we're all involved with.'

Naming no names as they were in a public place, Ivy was referring to Poppy Wilson.

Phoebe nodded, feeling light-headed with doubt and confusion and guilt. 'Yes. Zachary Archer,' she mumbled. 'He arrives this afternoon.'

And she'd have to drop her bombshell before he'd even had time to acclimatise.

Looking impressed, her friends stared as if waiting for her to elaborate. Only her mind blanked, stuck on how great a lover Zach had been and how she'd never once imagined when she'd invited him into her bed that she'd end up pregnant. Phoebe had long ago abandoned any dreams of motherhood, choosing instead to focus on her career, to devote her maternal impulses to her tiny patients.

'Have you two worked together before?' Harper prompted when Phoebe sat like a rabbit trapped in the headlights.

A question she could answer without being cagey!

'No. But his reputation in the field made him the first person I thought of to assist.' Poppy had been diagnosed with a large ventricular septal defect that had so far failed to close spontaneously, as often occurred. They wouldn't normally operate on a baby of her weight, but the hole in her heart was causing side effects that had so far proved resistant to medical intervention. Surgery was now the only option.

Oblivious to the sense of impending doom pounding Phoebe's heart at Zach's possible reactions, Ali asked, 'He's from Sydney, isn't he? He went to medical school with Jake,' she said about her new man.

'Yes, I believe so,' Phoebe said weakly. When she'd confided in Ali, she had refused to discuss the baby's father. It was only fair that she told

Zach first. 'But he's rarely here. He travels a lot, gets invited to centres all over the world to lend his expertise.'

Mentally calculating how many hours she might have before she saw him again, before she would have to impart her news, Phoebe wished she'd taken the coward's way out and informed him over the phone, or by email. But by the time she'd realised what her amenorrhoea and other symptoms meant, she'd already invited him to consult on the high-risk and highly publicised surgery. Then, when she'd confirmed her pregnancy with a test, it had made sense to wait for him to arrive in Sydney and tell him in person. Only now that the moment was almost upon her, she wanted to run away and hide from the inevitable conversation.

Swallowing, she pulled herself together. It wasn't as if she'd become pregnant on purpose, nor did she require anything of him beyond her obligation that he be informed.

'You look pale, Phoebs. Are you ill?' Harper said, eyeing Phoebe's untouched tea.

'I'm just tired,' she fudged, taking her first sip and trying not to wince at the unappealing taste. 'It's been a busy week.'

'Well at least my wedding gives us all something to look forward to,' Ivy said, turning the talk back to the main topic. 'It will be a chance for us all to get out of scrubs and get glammed up. Perhaps there'll be a dishy single guest we can hook you up with, Phoebs. That will put some colour back in your cheeks.'

Harper chuckled with Ivy, and Ali hid behind her coffee cup, avoiding comment. That was the trouble with loved-up friends, they turned into raging matchmakers, keen to spread the joy they'd found to anyone left single.

'You know me,' Phoebe said, reminding her friends of her fierce independence. 'I don't need a man.'

Because they'd heard Phoebe's mantra so many times, Ivy and Harper rolled their eyes, appeased for now. Only Ali, the woman in the know, still observed Phoebe with a small frown of concern that tightened the knot of nerves in Phoebe's stomach.

Was Ali imagining some sort of happy ending for sad spinster Phoebe? Did she think the baby's mystery father might sweep in to save the day and marry her poor, knocked-up friend?

Glancing away, Phoebe shuddered at the very idea. She had no intention of allowing her new life as a mother to be any different from her current self-sufficient existence. She was confident that she could handle one little baby without too much disruption to her schedule. She just needed to align all of her ducks, starting with informing Zach later today.

As if the universe had decided she'd already suffered enough probing questions for one day, Phoebe's phone pinged. She read the screen, relief flooding her system as she abandoned her tea and stood.

'Sorry, lovely ladies, I have to go. My first patient is being prepped. Hope you all have a good day.'

Rushing across the street to the hospital, she breathed a little easier. No matter what Ali thought, what Ivy and Harper might think once they knew of her pregnancy, Phoebe was happy to go it alone. She was a competent, capable medical professional, a mature, independent woman who didn't believe that happy endings necessitated falling in love. She would simply tell Zach her news, explain that she needed nothing from him, remind him that they'd both known that night in Brisbane was a no-strings, one-off arrangement and that nothing had changed. Once they'd operated together on Poppy Wilson, Zach could go his merry way and her normality could resume.

She had things all neatly figured out.

CHAPTER TWO

ZACH HELD HIS scrubbed clean and still dripping arms in front of him and placed his back against the scrub-room door, anticipation and excitement playing tug-of-war with his gut.

It had been three months but the memories of that night with Phoebe Mason had stayed fresh in his mind. When he'd received her email asking him to come to Sydney and consult on a high-profile and risky surgery, he'd been captivated at the idea of seeing her again, this time in her work environment.

Even before her request had come in some part of him had subconsciously hoped their paths would cross in the future. No matter how much he'd coached his thoughts after they'd slept together, adamant that their one night had been perfect, that Phoebe with her self-sufficiency and pragmatism and clear expectations was exactly the sort of woman he was drawn to, he couldn't scrub her from his mind.

And now he was about to see her again.

Pushing through the door into Theatre Three, Zach eagerly scanned the room. Despite the fact that she was scrubbed up, concealed from head to toe by forest-green surgical garments, he'd have known her anywhere. He recalled the sexy curves of her body, the elegant slope of her neck, the way she held her head as if she were a strict headmistress on the lookout for misbehaving children.

For a second she didn't notice his appearance, giving him a few moments to compose himself, breathe through the rush of adrenaline the sight of her caused. The last time he'd seen her, she'd been asleep on her stomach, her dark blonde hair splayed over the pillow, her back and shoulders bare, the white sheet bunched around her waist. He'd paused, marvelling at her beauty, desperate to trace the golden freckles that dotted her shoulders and follow the dip of her spine with his fingers, to lean forward and inhale the scent of her hair.

Now, dragging his gaze from her curves, he forced himself to shut down the reel of erotic memories from that unforgettable night.

He cleared his throat, alerting Phoebe and the scrub nurse to his presence.

Phoebe's bright blue eyes widened above her surgical mask, evidence of a blush visible on her high cheekbones. 'Dr Archer. What are you doing here? I wasn't expecting you until this afternoon.'

Her clipped, businesslike voice told him she intended to play their reunion cool.

He'd expected that. Each of them had made it clear that their one night in Brisbane wouldn't be repeated, but he couldn't help the sinking feeling in his stomach.

'Good morning, Dr Mason, good to see you again,' he said, taking a sterile towel from the theatre nurse to dry his hands and then donning sterile gloves and surgical apron.

'My apologies for surprising you,' he added, adjusting his gloves while the nurse tied the strings of the apron. Phoebe hadn't moved a muscle since she'd spied him, as if she was in shock. 'My flight arrived this morning, so rather than twiddle my thumbs, something I'm not very good at, I'm afraid, I thought I'd come in, acquaint myself with the set-up here at Sydney Central before our meeting.'

Phoebe stared, seeming more discombobulated than he'd anticipated. He hadn't meant to disrupt her day by showing up early and gatecrashing her surgery, he just struggled with idleness. The need to strive that he'd been raised with in his highly competitive family was a hard habit to break.

'I did clear it with the theatre manager. Didn't he tell you?' he said.

Still silent, Phoebe shook her head.

Zach clasped his gloved hands together in front

of him, a habit he'd developed as a medical student in order to remind himself not to touch anything once he was sterile. 'I can leave if it's a problem…'

Still looking at him as if he'd walked into this disinfected environment carrying an open vial of some deadly virus, she raised her chin a fraction. 'Well, I had planned for us to meet in my office later, but, as you're here, I'd be happy for you to stay and observe.'

She didn't sound at all happy.

Zach chuckled to himself, glad to see that the sparks they'd generated in Brisbane were still dangerously flammable.

'Good. Excellent.' Zach stood beside her to await the patient. He felt her stiffen as if he'd moved into her personal space, but they were most definitely a respectable distance apart. Interesting. Either she wanted to make it absolutely obvious that their physical relationship was over, or she was still reacting to him the way she had when they'd flirted in Brisbane, when her passion had matched his that night, kiss for kiss, touch for touch.

'So how have you been?' he asked, his voice low so they wouldn't be overheard by the theatre staff, who were bustling around preparing the OR for the first patient on Phoebe's operating list.

She needn't worry that he'd take her invitation

to jointly operate on Poppy Wilson as an invitation back into her bed. He wasn't about to cast aside his casual attitude to dating and swear her his undying love. He wasn't sure he even believed in the fickle emotion after the example he'd witnessed growing up, when, after having four children together, his parents decided that they could no longer tolerate the sight of each other.

'Well, thank you.' She kept her stare averted, the slightly strangled sound of her voice reminding him of her sexy moans and cries of passion as they'd surrendered to what had been insanely strong chemistry.

Now she was acting as if he had some sort of communicable disease, as if she regretted inviting him to corroborate on a ventricular septal defect surgery on the newborn daughter of local celebrity Aaron Wilson and his wife Emma.

Maybe joining her in Theatre had been a mistake. Only the minute he'd emerged from the shower after his long haul from London, impatience to see her again had gnawed at him, like hunger. He'd anticipated his ongoing attraction, expected some lively debates on their differing surgical approaches, looked forward to getting to know Phoebe a little better as a surgeon and woman he admired.

'Are you sure you have no objections to me

observing your surgery?' he asked, pretending to ignore her cool-as-a-cucumber act.

'None at all,' she said, glancing his way so he saw the glimmer of challenge in her eyes. 'Given that we're going to be corroborating on the Wilson case, it makes sense for us to get to know each other's surgical style, although, from the panel discussion in Brisbane, I'm certain that they will be wildly different.'

Zach chuckled. At least she'd brought up Brisbane so he didn't have to.

'Exactly my thought,' he said, enjoying the way she seemed flustered by his presence, but it seemed, would never admit it. 'Of course, we also proved in Brisbane that when it counts, we were able to find some…common ground.'

At the veiled innuendo he couldn't resist, Phoebe flushed. Zach smiled beneath his mask and, reading his expression, she shot him a look full of venom. He was irking her, but his trusted intuition told him that the woman she'd portrayed that night three months ago—the playful and passionate woman—was still there, underneath the distant and professional guard she had slammed up the minute he'd walked through the door.

And his gut feelings had never steered him wrong.

For reasons only known to Phoebe, she wanted to pretend that they hadn't spent the night pleasuring each other's bodies, that he didn't know every detail of how she looked naked, that their chemistry was a thing of the past. Like him, Phoebe liked to be in control and to call the shots, and, despite how those similarities led to the inevitable friction currently on display, he liked that aspect of her personality. He'd backed her into a corner by showing up early, but he had no doubt that if she wanted him to leave her OR, she would most definitely say.

Just then, Phoebe's tiny patient was wheeled into the OR by the anaesthetist.

Zach caught Phoebe's sigh of relief.

'So, tell me about your case?' he asked as he and Phoebe stood back to allow their colleagues to ready the patient for the impending surgery.

'It's a pretty standard, uncomplicated oesophageal atresia,' she said, looking up at him so he was bombarded anew by the way she had stood on tiptoes to kiss him. 'The patient is a three-day-old boy born at full term by normal vaginal delivery. Nothing to challenge your legendary skills, I'm sure.'

Zach shrugged, unperturbed by her attempts to chase him off. 'On the contrary,' he said, smiling. 'No case is too mundane to pique my interest. That's what makes me the best: attention to detail.'

She wasn't going to get rid of him that easily. Despite having no interest in dating, what with his workaholic tendencies, and not to mention his general cynicism towards commitment, he hadn't been able to get Phoebe off his mind since they slept together. As she was the first woman in years to provoke his fascination, he was more drawn to her than ever, even when her body language was practically shoving him out of the door.

'In that case,' she said as they took their positions opposite each other across the operating table, as if they'd worked together for years, 'I hope you feel my routine surgery makes your enthusiastic early appearance worthwhile.'

She looked up. Their eyes locked in challenge.

'I'm looking forward to it,' he said, his heart galloping because the sexual tension he'd assumed was one-sided seemed to have returned with a vengeance, mutual and stronger than before.

As Phoebe and the theatre nurse prepared the operative field with sterile surgical sheets, Zach's gaze stubbornly noticed the wisps of escaped hair caressing her neck below her hat and the way that her eyelashes seemed longer and lusher than he remembered. He couldn't help but tune into her every movement, to the soft sigh of her breathing and the scent of her subtle but highly distracting perfume.

Whatever happened between them during his short time in Sydney, it certainly wasn't going to be dull.

The emotion of facing Zach over a tiny baby she was about to operate on while, unbeknown to him, their own baby grew inside her rose up inside Phoebe, pressing on her lungs. She hadn't considered that Zach breezing into her OR early and unannounced would completely flummox and derail her. But his confident swagger, the heat and challenge in his stare—challenge she'd had no choice but to accept, given her stubborn streak—had brought a violent collision of her expectations and her stark reality.

Phoebe willed her breathing to slow. She couldn't have him thinking that his mere presence was enough to unsettle her equilibrium, to shock her system with delicious memories of the things they'd done together that night in Brisbane, to rouse her into another tit-for-tat verbal sparring match she could tell he'd enjoyed.

So he was even more attractive than her memory recalled, his shoulders impossibly broader, his height more impressive, his confidence hovering on the arrogant side of charismatic. It didn't matter that the minute he'd appeared in the OR her brain had shut down, instinct and hormones holding her body ransom so all she could think of was how it had felt the first time they'd kissed.

Because she was her mother's daughter, raised to live on her terms, Phoebe didn't do weakness. She wasn't about to start just because Zach liked to play by his own rules, appearing when it suited him rather than when he'd been invited. No doubt he'd leave in accordance with his own agenda, too.

Fine. That suited her down to the ground.

She'd tell him he was going to be a father, tolerate his irritating presence until they'd operated on Poppy, and then watch the trail of dust he would no doubt leave behind when he scarpered back overseas, never to be seen again. Just like her own father, who'd not only deserted Phoebe and her mother, but had blamed Rosa Mason for *trapping him into marriage.*

Ducking her head to avoid Zach's perceptive eye contact, she glanced at the anaesthetist, seeking the all-clear to proceed.

'We're good here,' said her colleague with a nod.

Shoving all thoughts of Zach and how effortlessly he'd rattled her from her mind, Phoebe reached for the scalpel from the tray of sterilised instruments. Instead of her fingers closing around the metal handle as she'd expected, she found herself gripping Zach's gloved hand.

She slammed her gaze to his, snatched her hand away. But it was too late. The warmth of his touch took her back to that night, to the way he'd worshipped her body all night long, telling her how beautiful she was and murmuring sexy things.

'Sorry.' He smiled, withdrawing his hand. 'Force of habit. I'm usually in the driving seat.'

Phoebe dragged in a steadying breath, desperately trying to ignore his imposing presence and the way he was looking at her as if their night together was at the foreground of his thoughts.

But of course he was used to running the show. She'd learned how he liked to take control in the bedroom when he'd commanded every kiss and touch, driving her body to the point of exhaustion with pleasure.

Trying to forget his prowess as a lover, she picked up the scalpel and cast him a withering look. 'Well, today I'm afraid you'll have to take the passenger seat.'

'I'm all yours, Dr Mason,' he said.

As she focused on her job and not the man opposite, the flustered gallop of her heart settled. She made an incision in the fourth right intercostal space and then prepared to enter the mediastinum, the surgical approach one she'd done a thousand times. Only never before watched by a man who'd not only seen her naked, but also kissed every inch of her body.

To her surprise, Zach stayed silent while she worked slowly and methodically to reach the unformed oesophagus. If she hadn't been so attuned to his proximity, as if her body's muscle memory sensed the source of all that pleasure was once more nearby, she might have forgotten he was there.

But she could tell that Zach was practically itching to get his hands on the instruments. Taking pity on him, she inserted a retractor into the incision she'd made into the chest cavity and passed it to him to hold. 'I can see that you're not very good at merely observing, Dr Archer.'

'You're right. I do like to have purpose, to know my role, whatever the situation, so thanks for putting me to use.'

Recalling how he'd put those hands to use, that mouth, when he'd driven her wild, she swallowed hard, her throat dry.

'Not good at being superfluous, then?' she asked, already certain of his response. Men like Zach—ambitious, overachieving perfectionists—measured their worth by their success. He was married to his work for a reason.

His emotional unavailability had been a major point in his favour when she had invited him into her bed. She had known exactly where she stood with him. Now that she was carrying their child, her expectations of him as a father were realistically negligible.

But Phoebe didn't need him for anything. She just needed to tie up the loose ends and tell him her secret.

'No, I'm afraid I was raised in a competitive household and have three high-achieving siblings. Fortunately for me that's translated into a world-leading career in a field that I love.'

Fascinated by his casual comment and the insight it gave her into his personality, Phoebe automatically adjusted the position of the retractor he held, a move that necessitated touching his warm and strong hand once more.

Impressed that a surgeon with Zach's pedigree was content to hold a retractor, a job traditionally undertaken by the most junior member of the surgical team, Phoebe smiled to herself, forced to re-examine his reputation for arrogance.

While the surgery progressed, she was constantly aware of Zach's scrutiny in the same way she'd been in Brisbane. She located the proximal blind end of the oesophagus, the normally patent tube that connected the mouth to the stomach, which in this case hadn't formed correctly so the baby couldn't feed. She created an opening in the tube so she could join the two ends of the oesophagus together. She was about to comment on how impressed she was that he'd managed to keep his criticisms of her surgical technique to himself, when he piped up.

'You have a bleeder,' he said, passing her the diathermy probe before she had a chance to reach for it.

'I see it,' she said, both grateful for a second pair of eyes, and irritated by his intrusion. She cauterised the tiny blood vessel, carefully moving aside the baby's lung to allow room for the suction tube.

That was when the cardiac monitor alarm blared its warning, and everyone froze.

The anaesthetist, who had been sitting at the head of the table, jerked to his feet and examined the heart trace spewed out by the cardiac monitor, which monitored the rate and rhythm of the heart.

Phoebe held her breath, her own heart rate through the roof. Peri-operative emergencies were a surgeon's worst nightmare, but never more so than when the patients were tiny, vulnerable, newborn babies.

As the alarm continued to sound, all eyes were glued to the digital reading of the heart trace on the monitor. The baby's heart was beating abnormally high.

Fighting off the instinctual panic the emergency warning created, Phoebe tried to set her emotions aside and think. There were many possible causes for the alarm, the most life-threatening a cardiac arrhythmia, which could be the result of the anaesthetic, the surgery or an undiagnosed issue with the heart's electrical conductive system. But whatever the cause, the surgery couldn't proceed until the episode was treated, or resolved spontaneously.

Adrenaline rushed through her blood. She glanced at Zach, saw the same concern and confusion in his eyes. Losing a patient on the table, while rare, was a heartbreaking reality of her job. She'd never grown used it and now that she was carrying her own child, it was as if the stakes were amplified tenfold.

Aware that she was senselessly projecting and that Zach was still ignorant of the existence of his child, a situation she vowed to rectify as soon as they'd finished this surgery, she looked away from him.

'Is it an arrhythmia?' she asked the anaesthetist, the seconds passing at the rate of what felt like hours while the alarm continued to blare out its warning.

Preoccupied, the anaesthetist shook his head. 'Looks like sinus tachycardia.'

'Why don't we check for pneumothorax?' Zach said, his stare transmitting his support.

Phoebe nodded, inspecting the operative field,

while Zach adjusted the position of the retractor to aid her view.

Every surgery carried risk. All surgeons worked with that knowledge. But this should have been a routine procedure.

As quickly as it had begun, the heart rate settled to normal, the alarm falling silent. Phoebe battled hand tremors as her adrenaline dissipated, leaving only the alien sense of gratitude for Zach's calming and supportive presence.

Refusing to be complacent, Phoebe said, 'Let's double-check that there's no pneumothorax and that I didn't miss another bleeder.'

Nodding, Zach assisted, inspecting the chest cavity for signs of surgical complications, while the anaesthetist monitored the baby's blood pressure, respiratory rate and other vital signs, which to everyone's collective relief remained stable.

'It looks good to me, Dr Mason,' Zach said when Phoebe had checked every nook and cranny of the operative field, twice.

Phoebe nodded. 'Are you happy for us to proceed?' she asked the anaesthetist, who gave her the all-clear once more.

The rest of the surgery passed uneventfully, but the minute Phoebe sneaked away to the female changing rooms, she braced her hands on her thighs and bent double, releasing the tension caused by the emergency that had taken place with every deep inhale and exhale.

With her panic subsided, another realisation struck.

Despite the fact that he'd joined her surgery, uninvited, despite the fact that she was glad he'd been there, the time to confess her bombshell had arrived. When it mattered, it seemed she and Zach might be able to set aside their personal life and work together, successfully. It not only benefited their last patient, but boded well for Poppy Wilson, too.

Unless, when she told him her news, everything changed.

CHAPTER THREE

STRAIGHTENING HIS TIE and rolling back his shoulders, Zach tapped on the already ajar door bearing Phoebe's name and poked his head through the opening.

'Come in.' Phoebe beckoned him, smoothing her hand over her neatly pulled-back hair in a nervous gesture.

She looked pale. Zach wondered if she'd been spooked by the emergency in the OR or if she was still regretting inviting him to the Central.

'Hi.' Zach smiled, hoping that, as mature professional adults, they could fully dispense with the awkwardness of earlier. After all, sex was just sex, even when it had been the best sex of his life, and they'd proved that, despite being former lovers, they had worked well together on the oesophageal atresia surgery.

Phoebe was a meticulous surgeon, handling the unforeseen emergency with impressive calm that only inflamed Zach's attraction to her further. All surgeons dreaded the sound of those alarms, although sometimes, like in that case, the cause for a raised heart rate or drop in blood pressure never became apparent. Even so, he'd admired the way Phoebe had checked twice before proceeding with the operation. It showed a humility that he couldn't help but respect.

Still eyeing him warily, Phoebe stood as Zach left the door ajar and stepped further into her office. She'd replaced the hospital's green scrubs with an immaculate charcoal trouser suit that cinched in at the waist and accentuated her figure. The sage-green blouse made her blue eyes a shade brighter, but her expression was distant. Physically, she took his breath away. But despite the time they'd spent together in Brisbane, she seemed determined to demarcate boundaries, her body language making it clear that they would be staying on opposite sides of her clutter-free, blond oak desk.

His heart sank.

Clearly the easy-going reunion he'd imagined wasn't going to become a reality.

'Have a seat.' She indicated the lone chair facing hers, no hint of the warmth he'd hoped to coax out now that they were alone.

Zach hesitated, irked that their first private interaction since he'd forced himself to leave her warm hotel room bed while she slept naked would feel like a job interview.

'How are you feeling now?' he asked, instead of sitting. 'That turned out to be far from the run-of-the-mill surgery you promised.' He flashed his cheeky smile, the one his mother claimed had saved him from trouble on more than one occasion as a kid, trying to lighten the atmosphere in the hope that she'd drop her guard a little.

'I'm fine, thank you.' Looking away, she took a seat, straightened the pen on her desk, once more stroked her hair. 'Yes, things did get rather fraught there for a minute, just to keep us on our toes.'

When she looked up, the briefest hint of vulnerability flared in her eyes. It gave him hope that, as he'd predicted, the Phoebe he'd spent the night with in Brisbane was hiding somewhere behind this buttoned-up, untouchable and aloof version.

The question was, why?

Making one last attempt to break the ice, Zach gestured at the open door. 'I hoped we could catch up over coffee. I noticed a popular café across the road,' he said, hoping to chip away at her frosty resistance.

Away from her work environment, perhaps they could have a genuine conversation, two mature adults who knew the intimacies of each other's bodies, respected each other professionally, and still had to work together.

Her teeth snagged at her full bottom lip, reminding him of her kisses, her sighs, the sexy
things she'd said when they'd been intimate.
'I'm…um…off coffee at the moment. It's a de-
tox-challenge thing going around the hospital.'

She flushed, glancing away, and Zach decided
enough was enough. They didn't know each other
well, but neither were they strangers. She'd invited him here and now she was acting as if she
couldn't wait for him to leave.

Time to clear the air.

'Look—' Zach stifled a sigh and took the prof-
fered seat. 'Am I making you uncomfortable or
something? Did I upset you by inserting myself
into your OR? Because I apologise for that.'

She shook her head. 'I'm not upset. I'm glad
you were there.' Her clear gaze meeting his, for
the first time open. 'I'm also grateful that you're
able to consult on the Poppy Wilson case. I know
you're in high demand and, given what happened
in Brisbane, I wondered if you might decline for
personal reasons. But, like me, you've put all of
that behind us.' She waved her hand dismissively.
'Which is great.'

Yeah…really great…

Zach frowned at her prepared-sounding
speech, torn because he respected her for raising the subject of Brisbane. But who was she
trying to convince that all that messy physical

attraction was in the past—him or herself? For
Zach, chemistry as strong as theirs was almost
impossible to ignore.

'By "all of that", I assume you mean the four
times we had sex?' It was a low blow, but the part
of him that had been desperate to see her again
couldn't resist reminding her how good they'd
been together.

'Yes.' She swallowed hard, nodded absently,
the exposed skin in the vee neck of her blouse
turning pink.

Relieved to know that she wasn't as unaffected
as she'd have him believe, but feeling uncharac-
teristically irritated, as if he was being somehow
managed—a situation for which he had no toler-
ance—he leaned back in the chair and rested his
ankle on the opposite knee.

'I'm a professional, Phoebe. I'd never allow
sexual chemistry to interfere with work.' Even
when, for him, that chemistry was as rampant as
ever, maybe even more so than before because of
the three months of anticipation.

'Exactly,' she said in a tone that implied that
part of the conversation was over. Composing
herself, she donned her glasses and logged into
the computer. 'So, let's get you up to speed on
Poppy Wilson, shall we?'

She angled the monitor his way so they could
both see the screen, clearly still keen to keep him

physically separated, when he would have preferred to share the same side of the desk.

Feeling mildly dismissed by work Phoebe, Zach clenched his jaw and nodded for her to proceed. Where was the woman he'd struggled to forget, the woman who'd flirted, seduced him and passionately shattered in his arms?

While she outlined Poppy's medical history following her birth at thirty-two weeks gestation by uncomplicated caesarean section, Zach tried to ignore the sensual way her mouth moved. The trouble was, the urge to kiss her again beat at him relentlessly, like a wasp flying at an unopened window.

And the attraction was most definitely mutual. He hadn't missed the way her stare had checked him out when he'd entered her office, the way she touched her neck every time their eyes met. Why had she locked herself away behind this fortress of polite professionalism, especially now that they were alone? And more disturbingly, why was he allowing it to get to him?

He should feel relieved that she knew what she wanted and had stated it so honestly that night in Brisbane. Working together with all of that chemistry flying around had the potential for them to be tempted into another liaison. At least this way, with Phoebe making it abundantly clear that, beyond needing his assistance on this high-profile surgery, their association was over, kept things simple, something he normally sought out.

'So unless you have any objections,' she said, bringing him back to the surgical plan for Poppy, 'I propose that we use a traditional open surgical procedure via the right atrium approach and a synthetic patch. Would you like to see the echocardiogram?'

'I would,' Zach said, standing and coming around to her side of the desk, uninvited, so he could gain a closer look at the images on the screen. If their attraction was now one-sided—if, for her, he was just any other colleague—she wouldn't be at all bothered by his proximity.

'I can turn the monitor around,' she flustered, opening a new screen to show him the Doppler scan, which would likely illustrate the abnormal flow of blood through the defect in the inter-ventricular wall of Poppy's heart.

'It's no problem,' Zach said, bending over her shoulder, his determination to prove his point backfiring as a cloud of her floral scent engulfed him, making it hard for him to think about anything but the fact that when he'd left her bed after that night, her scent had clung to his skin. 'I do my best thinking on my feet,' he added, 'and this way, we can both see without craning our necks.'

She stiffened as he rested his hand on the back of her chair and peered at the screen. While he watched the images, Phoebe touched her throat nervously, toyed with the thin gold chain she wore around her neck.

As much as he wanted to give her a little nudge out of her comfort zone and have her admit that she too still felt this thing bubbling away between them, Zach backed off. He'd had his fun with Phoebe and he'd seen what he needed to see from the scan pictures.

Now he'd just have to focus on the job, try to ignore his ongoing attraction and console himself that whatever dreams he might have subconsciously harboured about them hooking up once more were never going to happen.

Before he could retake his seat on the other side of the desk, Phoebe's face drained of colour. She placed a hand on her forehead, her other hand gripping the arm of her leather chair.

Alarmed by her pallor, Zach rushed back to her side. 'Phoebe, are you okay?'

The doctor in him couldn't help but reach for her radial pulse at her wrist, which was steady but a little fast.

'Just a bit a dizzy,' she muttered. 'I didn't eat much breakfast.'

She pushed her chair away from the desk and dropped her head between her knees. 'I'll be fine.' Her voice was muffled. 'I'll see you later.'

Even dizzy she was still trying to get rid of

him. Clearly she was feeling unwell. He couldn't just leave her like this.

'I'm not leaving until I know you're okay,' he said, restless with concern and frustration that her independent streak seemed to be a mile wide. 'Tell me what I can do for you. Do you want a glass of water? Some food from the canteen?'

He curled his fingers into useless fists, his protective urges, the need to act, to fix whatever had crept up on her leaving him rigid with impotence.

Why wouldn't she accept his help?

'Can you please page Dr Ali Edwards?' she said eventually. 'She's a friend of mine who works here.'

Reaching for the desk phone, Zach made the call to the hospital switchboard to summon Phoebe's friend. When he hung up, he persuaded her that it might help if she lay on the sofa. He scooped one arm around her waist, guiding her unsteadily to lie down. Then he removed her shoes and propped her feet up on the arm of the sofa in order to redirect blood back to her head.

She was still pale, her dark lashes stark on her cheeks where she kept her eyes closed. Zach paced, his heart frantic behind his ribs. Perhaps she'd been more upset by the emergency in Theatre this morning than she'd let on.

'I'm okay now,' she said, cracking open one eye to look up at him. 'Thank you.'

Her colour had returning slightly, so he collected a glass of water from the sink in the corner of the room and helped her back into a sitting position. 'You should always eat a decent breakfast,' he said, handing her the glass, 'especially before a surgical list.'

He didn't mean to sound patronising, but she'd scared him. The way she'd clung to his hand, rested her weight against his side while he'd walked her to the sofa, the biggest shock of all. Phoebe was the most self-sufficient woman he'd ever known. Certainly the Phoebe he'd encountered this morning would only have leaned on him if absolutely necessary.

Phoebe had barely taken two sips of water when a tall woman with black curly hair and big brown eyes, which were etched with concern, entered the room, slightly out of breath.

'Are you okay?' She rushed to Phoebe with only a cursory glance Zach's way, automatically taking her friend's pulse, as Zach had done.

'Fine,' Phoebe mumbled. 'I just felt a little bit faint. I'm okay.' She looked up at Zach as if she wanted to say more but needed him to leave first.

Zach shoved his hands in his pockets, helplessness a tight knot in his stomach. Perhaps he should give the friends some privacy. He would leave, but not before ensuring that Phoebe was truly okay and not simply putting on a show of independence for his benefit.

As if remembering social etiquette, Phoebe made introductions. 'Ali, this is Zachary Archer. He'll be operating with me on Poppy Wilson. Zach, this is my friend Ali Edwards, Head of Obstetrics and Gynaecology here at Sydney Central.'

Relief drained through his body. At least Phoebe was speaking, feeling well enough to ensure everyone understood that they were just colleagues.

Ali briefly nodded at Zach and then turned her attention back to Phoebe. 'I'd like to take your blood pressure. There's a sphyg in the examination room next door.'

Zach liked Ali Edwards already. She seemed to be taking no nonsense from her friend.

To his surprise, Phoebe nodded compliantly, shooting Zach another wary glance, this one tinged with what looked like fear.

Was she scared of him?

She stood, her shoulders slumped as if weighed down with a sense of inevitability.

Zach held his breath, held his ground, trepidation building inside him like a head of steam. What on earth was going on here? He wasn't leaving until he understood.

Phoebe squeezed Ali's arm. 'I'll meet you next door in a second.'

Ali hesitated, glancing his way with a frown Zach was certain must be mirrored in his own expression.

Seeing that her friend was reluctant to leave her alone with him, Phoebe urged, 'I'm fine, Ali. I just need to talk to Zach, alone.'

Her voice was strong once more and full of determination, her cryptic statement making Zach's skin prickle with a sense of foreboding.

CHAPTER FOUR

WHILE HER HEART pounded away behind her ribs, Phoebe held Zach's quizzical and intense stare, feeling utterly exposed.

Her dizzy spell had arrived with impeccable timing, her moment of weakness in front of him even now making her desperate to be alone, to have him leave, to stop looking at her with worry and confusion that somehow only added to the weight of her secret.

Because she was swamped by guilt.

The moment had come, snatched out of her control by the events of the morning—being caught off guard by his unscheduled appearance, the emergency in Theatre, which only added to her sense of vulnerability and the effects of the pregnancy hormones hijacking her body.

Ali closed the door and Phoebe looked down at her twisted hands, away from Zach's searching expression. 'Sorry about that.' She cleared her throat, needing to sound as in control as she'd planned. 'I um…need to tell you something.'

She couldn't have him finding out that he was going to be a father in front of Ali. She owed him some prior warning, some privacy in the moment. It was bound to be as much a shock for Zach as it had been for her.

Taking in his worry-etched face, she winced. She should have ripped off the plaster, told him the minute he'd walked into her office, the minute he'd walked into Theatre even. But he'd looked so handsome in his midnight-blue suit, looking at her as if he wanted to be back in that hotel room in Brisbane, as if he wanted to slide his fingers into her hair and tilt her face up to his kiss, that she'd been overcome by a wave of lust and gratitude that he'd helped her finish the oesophageal atresia surgery and she'd bungled her well-prepared speech.

Zach's frown deepened. He shoved his hands in his trouser pockets, defensively. 'Okay, I'm listening.'

Perching on the edge of her desk, she wiped her sweaty palms down the legs of her trousers. She was making such a mess of this, when in her head her confession had been succinct, unemotional, a done deal whereby she would have been in control.

Only now, she was all over the place.

'Um…about Brisbane,' she said, gnawing at her lip. If she'd done this over the phone, or via email, she'd have avoided having to look at him while she imparted her life-altering news. She didn't know Zach well enough to know how he'd react. But she wasn't a coward and the minute she told him he'd likely want as little to do with her as possible, so it really didn't matter.

'I thought we'd put Brisbane behind us,' he said, throwing her words from earlier back in her face.

He seemed miffed, as if he'd expected something more from their reunion. But surely he hadn't imagined they would pick up where they left off? He'd been as adamant as her that it was a one-night deal.

'I did say that.' Phoebe nodded, gripping the edge of her desk. Hysterical, inappropriate laughter clogged her throat. Was he under the impression that she wanted to talk about the best sex of her life, when she'd worked hard since the next day to forget it?

There was no way to soften the blow, and the longer she dithered, the harder it was to say the words. She dragged in a breath and simply blurted it out. 'I have put it behind me, but the thing is I'm pregnant.'

Now that she'd dropped her bombshell, relief forced her to exhale a long sigh.

She waited, sympathetic to his confused reaction.

Zach's frown intensified, deep grooves etched between his brows as his eyes darted over her face. He was trying to judge if she was joking, no doubt. 'We used condoms.'

Expecting his disbelief, she nodded, trying to dim the recollections from that incredible night where once they'd touched each other, they hadn't been able to stop.

She'd never been so insatiable for anyone before, and Zach had seemed equally ardent.

'I know,' she said. 'One of them didn't work.' Compassion for him swelled in her chest. Of course he'd experience the same shock she had when she'd seen that telltale pink line on the pregnancy test. She'd had over a month to get used to the idea.

He stood stock-still, his arms now hanging by his sides, his eyelids blinking occasionally the only part of him to move.

Phoebe winced, taking pity on him, rushing ahead to the reassurance part of her speech. 'The thing is, I thought you should know, but I don't need anything from you.'

His eyes darkened, bewilderment and anger warring for control of his expression. 'But it took you, what, two months to tell me?'

Caught red-handed, Phoebe fidgeted with her necklace. 'I didn't realise myself for the first two months. I've never had a regular cycle. Then, when it was confirmed, I… I thought it was best to tell you in person,'

As if deaf to her reasonable explanation, he gripped the back of his neck and paced towards the door, spinning once he ran out of carpet. 'Hold on, did you lure me here, invite me to Sydney on the pretext of needing my help with a surgery just to drop this in my lap?'

Phoebe bristled, appalled. 'No! The timing of my discovery around the same time I invited you here to consult on Poppy Wilson's surgery was coincidental, not manufactured, I assure you. I didn't want to tell you by email or even on the phone, and I figured as you'd agreed to come anyway, I could wait and tell you face to face.'

Zach held up one hand, cutting off her explanation. 'So in summary, just so I understand: you wanted me to know that in six months' time I'm going to be a father, but you don't need me to be involved, in fact, it probably suits you best if I'm not. Do I have that right? Have I missed anything?'

Queasy with nerves and guilt, drained from the emotions of the morning and a little embarrassed that she'd not only almost fainted in front of him, but also messed up her grand declaration, Phoebe blustered, 'I mean, I want the baby to know its father—'

'Well, that's something, I guess,' he interrupted, his lips thinned with annoyance.

How had she managed to offend him so deeply? This had gone much better in her head, where they'd had endless mature, respectful versions of this conversation. But perhaps that was the point. She'd had time to prepare, and he was understandably shell-shocked.

'What I mean is,' she rushed on, hoping that they could get the matter cleared up before her clinic began in thirty minutes, 'we both knew in Brisbane that neither of us was looking for any kind of relationship or commitment, and this pregnancy...' she placed her hand over her still-flat stomach '...changes nothing.'

Zach looked as if he was about to argue the point, his gaze resting where her hand was for a second. In a moment of insanity, Phoebe imagined him dropping to his knee, producing a ring and frogmarching her down the aisle.

She shuddered at the ridiculous and implausible thought. Zach looked as if he regretted ever meeting her, and she had no intention of confusing lust for love, if that even existed. Having a child together certainly wasn't enough to keep her own parents together. In fact, her father had used Phoebe as his argument for leaving, saying he'd felt trapped, as if he hadn't been an active participant in his own wedding and Phoebe's conception.

Proposals! Huh—she'd spent too much time surrounded by her loved-up friends.

As if on cue, Ali popped her head around the door, her curious gaze darting between Phoebe and Zach. 'Um… Ready when you are, Phoebs.'

Phoebe nodded and sighed, a tension headache forming. Ali had no idea that Zach was the father—no one knew. But her astute friend must be dying with curiosity given recent events.

This was turning into an uncontrollable nightmare.

Taking in their expressions, Zach's stony and Phoebe's no doubt defensive, and clearly cognisant of the tension in the room, Ali glanced at Zach uncertainly. 'I'll um… just wait then, shall I?'

Phoebe dithered, uncertain what to do next. She wanted to check that all was well with the baby after her near faint and she knew Ali always carried a portable foetal Doppler heart ultrasound in her pocket. But should she invite Zach into the examination? She'd assumed that he would have heard her news and have stomped away by now.

Instead, he turned to Ali, taking control of the conversation. 'I'd like to be present. If it's okay with you,' he said, turning back to Phoebe.

Completely thrown by the determination of

his request, and with two pairs of eyes awaiting her approval, all Phoebe could do was nod and follow Ali into the examination room next door, a silent and brooding Zach bringing up the rear.

As he closed the door to the examination room behind them, Phoebe's friend Ali glanced over at Zach, her eyes practically on stalks with curiosity. Still reeling from Phoebe's shock announcement, still processing the flutter of bemused excitement making it hard to draw a deep breath, Zach looked to Phoebe for his cue. He had no idea how much Phoebe had confided to her friend. Perhaps no one knew that she was pregnant. Perhaps Phoebe didn't want anyone to know that *he* was the father. But he had rights too, and being out of control, being uncertain of his role, was not a situation that suited Zach's personality.

Then he spied a portable ultrasound machine in the corner and clenched his jaw. Confused and annoyed that he might have been the last to know about the pregnancy, he breathed through the impulse to set the record straight to Phoebe's friend.

I've just found out I'm the father of this baby.

We hooked up once and I'd been hoping we might again, but she's been keeping this from me.

No, we're not together and Phoebe can't wait to get rid of me because she can do all of this alone.

Deciding to leave the explanations up to Phoebe, Zach focused on his breathing. His hands were trembling. He was going to be a father. Was the baby okay? Did Phoebe's dizziness mean something was wrong?

'Ali…' Phoebe said as she climbed onto the examination couch and waved her hand vaguely in his direction, 'Zach is…um…the father.'

Ali quickly contained her surprise, schooling her expression into a serene smile he assumed was her consultation face.

'Yes,' Zach said, sticking out his hand for a handshake as if they were any other excited expectant couple here for their first check-up. Except they weren't a couple. And from Phoebe's actions this morning, which in light of her news now made perfect sense, from what she'd said about needing nothing from him, it was barndoor obvious that they never would be.

'So you already know that Phoebe is pregnant?' he asked, swallowing the renewed pang of disappointment he'd experienced when faced with Phoebe's distant attitude. It wasn't as if he'd been about to propose to her, but the fact that she not only considered him superfluous, but had also kept him in the dark about his baby while confiding in her friends made his hackles rise. For a high achiever who took charge of every aspect of his life, the lack of control, the insignificance, was as intolerable as it was alien.

Ali had the good grace to flash him an apologetic look. 'Um…yes. I learned the wonderful news recently. Congratulations.' She beamed while she fastened the blood-pressure cuff around Phoebe's arm.

Zach deflated. This woman was an obstetrician, qualified to advise and care for Phoebe and their unborn baby. Part of him was grateful that she'd known about his baby before him.

Phoebe sagged back against the pillows, eyeing Zach warily. 'Now that we've done the introductions, can we please do this? I have clinic soon.'

'So you two met in Brisbane,' Ali fished as she removed the blood-pressure cuff and added to Phoebe, 'Your blood pressure is normal, by the way.'

The word *met* could clearly be substituted for *hooked up*.

'Yes.' Phoebe flushed, telling Zach what he'd already guessed at: that Phoebe had most likely told her friends nothing after Brisbane. That she obviously considered Zach a footnote in the story, someone she'd have never thought about again without this unforeseen consequence of their night together. To independent Phoebe he was irrelevant, just a man who'd inadvertently provided sperm.

This was why he didn't trust relationships. People were all about their own agenda, he'd seen that when his parents' marriage had crumbled and they'd gone from a loving couple with four children to two individuals who suddenly couldn't stand each other.

'Wonderful,' Ali said, smiling at Zach as if he might be the man of Phoebe's dreams.

Zach bit his tongue. There was no such man. Phoebe had made it clear just now, and by her reluctance to tell him straight away, that she needed Zach as much as she needed a six-month supply of alcohol.

'Neither of us wants a relationship.' Phoebe rushed to clarify, as good as telling her friend to forget whatever romantic ideas were putting that fascinated excitement in her eyes. 'It was a one-night thing.'

'In fact, you knew about my baby before I did,' Zach added, pointedly, 'as I've literally just been informed.' Zach clenched his jaw, because Phoebe was right. He'd always enjoyed his life the way it was, his relationships casual. Anything more required feelings, and Zach knew from the disaster his parents had made of their marriage that feelings, love, never lasted, even when you'd been committed for years and had a family.

But that was before.

Having taken years of flak from his parents

and siblings for his single, childless status, he'd never once imagined that he'd have a baby of his own. Except it was happening.

Phoebe stared daggers his way, likely because she'd already explained that she'd intended to tell him in person, hence the delay. But he wasn't feeling reasonable. He'd been manipulated and dismissed, given no time to come to terms with the fact that his life was changed for ever.

Aware of the drop in temperature in the room, Ali busied herself with the scan, changing the subject with true professionalism. 'My registrar wheeled over the ultrasound machine, so let's see if we can see the little one, shall we?'

Phoebe exposed her abdomen and Ali squirted on some ultrasound gel. Ali positioned the scan wand over Phoebe's lower abdomen and moved it around, pressing buttons to alter the image resolution as she peered closely for signs of a foetal sac.

Zach stared at the grainy image on the screen, his heart thudding in his throat with anticipation. He'd just been told the news and now he was about to see his baby for the first time. Trying to grapple with it all made his head spin.

With another click, the screen froze on an image of his and Phoebe's baby.

Zach stilled, time slowing. He stared in utter wonder at the baby's head, the heart, the arms and legs. It was a miracle, one he'd always respected, given his occupation, but now he was looking at his own baby.

He was going to be a father.

A hot lump of emotion lodged in his throat and he instantly knew he would walk over burning coals to meet any need their baby might have, now or in the future. Stunned, he glanced at Phoebe, who was staring too. She might not have even been aware of it, but her hand was gripping his arm so tight, he wondered how he'd missed her touching him.

Ali pressed another button and the image switched back to real time, only now there was sound, the rapid flutter of the heartbeat they could clearly see on the screen.

A surge of protective love eclipsed every other thought in Zach's head.

'Is everything all right?' Phoebe asked, releasing Zach as Ali handed them each a printed photo of their tiny baby.

Dazed, Zach scoured the photo and perched on the foot of the examination couch before he fell to his knees.

'Everything seems perfectly normal,' Ali said, replacing the wand and handing Phoebe a box of tissues so she could clean up.

'As a doctor,' Ali said, 'I'm recommending that you try to eat regularly. I know it's hard with the morning sickness, but we don't want any more fainting spells, do we?'

Phoebe nodded her agreement, zipping up her trousers. 'I'll grab something before my clinic begins.'

Ali glanced Zach's way once more, her smile now full of sympathy that made him feel somehow insignificant, as if she too suspected he wouldn't be in the picture for long.

'I'll leave you two to talk,' she said and quietly left the room.

Silence bellowed in his head as he placed the precious scan photo in his inside jacket pocket.

Phoebe was carrying his baby. Phoebe wanted nothing from him.

He looked at her, desperate for a cue on what he was supposed to say, how he was supposed to act, for the first time in his life—a life of constantly striving, of focusing solely on his work and trusting his instincts, the strength of his convictions unwavering—totally and utterly lost.

CHAPTER FIVE

PHOEBE STARED AT ZACH, her heart skipping a beat with compassion at his bewildered expression. She'd only ever seen him supremely confident, decisive, certain in his ability to command his own universe. Now his stunned expression brought her hot shameful guilt for not telling him sooner bubbling to the surface. She'd had weeks to come to terms with the life-changing news she'd literally just dropped in his lap. She herself was still reeling from seeing their baby for the first time.

As she glanced down at the scan picture once more, Phoebe's jaw dropped in wonder. She was mesmerised by the image. Until the moment she'd seen their baby's tiny heart beat on the screen, she'd half believed that the multiple tests she'd performed, the amenorrhoea and the pregnancy symptoms were all imagined somehow. But now that she'd seen the proof with her own eyes, held photographic evidence in her hand, a wave of love washed over her as reality dawned.

This was truly happening. She was going to be a mother.

Wanting to reassure Zach, she swung her legs over the edge of the examination couch so they sat side by side. 'Look, Zach, it's okay. However you're feeling is fine, honestly. I'm still a little overwhelmed by all of this myself, so I understand.'

She'd watched his earlier confusion morph to disbelief and then annoyance and return full circle back to confusion. She'd cycled through the same raft of emotions when she'd first found out.

Zach scrubbed a hand over his face as if he could snap himself out of the shock. 'I don't know how I'm feeling, to be honest.'

Phoebe nodded, caught off guard by his vulnerability and his honest admission. She wanted to touch him, to take his hand and comfort him, but she wasn't certain her gesture would be welcome. She didn't know this version of Zach and the man who'd swanned into her OR, into her office earlier, flashing his sexy smile and playing havoc with her hormones was understandably nowhere to be seen.

'That's okay too,' she said, her voice soft and patient. 'It's a lot to take in.' Realising that the joy of the moment was ever so slightly dampened for her too, because she couldn't share it with him the way she would if they were a couple—laughter through tears, a hug, a kiss, staring at the grainy image together while they held hands—Phoebe supressed the urge to reach out to him, physically.

They'd made this baby together during a night of incredible passion. And while she'd waited for the scan confirmation that all was well from Ali, her first instinct had been to reach for Zach. She'd acted on autopilot, needing some contact in case he'd been feeling as nervous as her, but also needing the connection for her own comfort. Somewhere in the deep recesses of her mind, she'd known that they were in this together.

Now that the moment had passed, she drew on her self-sufficiency once more.

'Look,' she continued, hoping to set his mind at ease, 'I have absolutely zero expectations of you. Having this baby was *my* decision. I know how much you travel with your work, so of course I don't expect you to be around. I'm perfectly happy doing this on my own. My mother was a single parent, raised me alone, so I've had a great role model. I'm confident that I'll do as good a job of raising our baby.'

At Zach's continued silence, which in itself was fairly worrying for a man so self-assured, she rambled on. 'Honestly, I have everything figured out.'

She was a busy professional career woman.

She could slot one little baby into her life, no problem.

'Ask my friends,' she continued. 'I am the queen of lists, super-organised. This isn't going to change me in the slightest.'

Still quiet, Zach shifted beside her. Growing aware of his closeness, of the way her body naturally leaned in his direction, of his delicious manly scent and the way her gaze more often than not landed on his mouth when she looked at him, Phoebe was forced to admit that she was still helplessly drawn to his charisma, intelligence, not to mention astounding physicality.

But she'd get over her attraction, which was likely a product of her pregnancy hormones. Once he left Sydney, she'd no longer have that confusing distraction.

'And of course,' she continued, 'whenever you're back in Sydney you're welcome to visit the baby. If you give me a picture of yourself, I'll keep it in the nursery, talk about you all the time so the baby grows up knowing who you are.'

Her concern that he remained mute was becoming quite alarming. If he'd only say something, anything, she'd know that he was okay.

As if the universe had heard her request, Zach pulled his vibrating phone from his pocket and glanced down at the screen. 'I have to go,' he said, tucking his phone into his jacket and standing.

'Oh, of course.' Phoebe shrugged on her professional demeanour to match Zach's business-like tone. She exhaled, glad that the worst was over. Duty done, she'd informed Zach that their night in Brisbane had produced consequences and, aside from his understandable shock, everything seemed to be going to plan.

Phoebe stood, buttoning up her jacket and straightening her hair. 'Me too, actually. My clinic is about to start.'

Despite the way she'd bungled her announcement, this was now going exactly the way she'd planned. So why, as she faced him, did a trickle of silly disappointment sneak under her guard?

Zach stared back, his expression inscrutable. Phoebe tried not to squirm, chewing her lip. She blinked away the silly burning sensation behind her eyes. Surely she wasn't hoping that he'd want to be a part of their lives, hers and the baby's? She had first-hand experience of how wrong things could go when one person in a relationship felt trapped. Her father had readily moved to the town where Phoebe's mother had grown up and then later resented his choice.

'Is there a canteen in the hospital?' he asked, the abrupt change of topic taking her by surprise.

'Um, yes. It's on the fourth floor, directly above us.'

He nodded, looking more like his old self. 'Are you free tonight?'

Another subject switch. Phoebe's head was beginning to spin.

'Um…'

'I think we should talk,' he said, his voice persuasive bordering on inflexible, as if he was back in control. 'We need to have an adult conversation about this, away from the hospital when neither of us is rushed.'

She nodded, unable to argue with his calm logic, or the determination in the set of his jaw. 'Yes, of course. I'll be finished here by six thirty.'

This was good. Once they'd settled all of the details like adults, once Zach had had a chance to come to terms with the news and ask any questions he might have, they could move on and life would get back to normal, exactly what she wanted.

'Perfect—I'll meet you back here at six-thirty.' He straightened his tie, which somewhere along the way during the past forty minutes had become ever so slightly askew.

'But first,' he added, his voice clipped, decisive in a way that reminded Phoebe of their difference of opinion on the panel discussion at the Brisbane conference, 'I'm going upstairs to buy you some lunch, which I'll leave with your clinic receptionist. No arguments.'

He moved to the door, glanced over his shoulder one last time, his stare sweeping over her from head to toe so that, when he left the room, she collapsed back onto the couch and dragged in a few calming breaths, both annoyed at his high-handedness and horribly turned on.

Running a shaky hand over her hair, she had time for only one thought as she rushed to her clinic: *That went as well as could be expected.*

CHAPTER SIX

ZACH DISLIKED NOTHING more than being caught in the fork of an impossible choice. It reminded him of his parents' messy divorce and the way they'd appointed him go-between. Sitting opposite Phoebe at Tutto Bene, the small casual Italian restaurant close to the hospital, later that evening, with her news and her subsequent dismissal still spinning in his head as if his brain were buffering, Zach feared that whatever happened tonight would trigger his most deeply ingrained insecurity: failing.

Glancing away from Phoebe, who was perusing the menu, he forced himself to stop staring. He'd thought she was beautiful before he'd known about the pregnancy, but now she seemed to glow from within, her skin softer looking, her hair more luxurious than he remembered. Even her voice seemed to carry a hint of new contentment.

But his continuing attraction and renewed fascination with the woman who had occupied his thoughts since Brisbane was completely irrelevant.

All that mattered now was the well-being of her and their baby.

Swallowing down the foreign taste of doubt, Zach reasoned his current position, where Phoebe had dropped her bombshell and then deemed him superfluous, was precisely the reason he'd always avoided the commitment of a serious relationship all these years. Zach didn't do failure. In avoiding emotional entanglement, he'd been able to focus solely on his career, his work ethic a result of being raised in a family encouraged to aim for the stars.

And while, now he was an adult, the constant rivalry between him, his two older brothers and his older sister drove him mad, something he avoided engaging in if at all possible, his life choices had also become a point of one-upmanship. He was the only unmarried sibling, the only one without children.

Until now. Now he was going to be a father...

'I'm starving,' Phoebe said, snatching him from the memory of how, needing to clear his head and come to terms with the shock news, Zach had cancelled his meeting at Nurture, the neonatal charity he often worked for, thrown on his running gear and pounded out twenty-five kilometres along the shoreline before he was able to rationalise his turbulent thoughts. As he'd bent double to catch his breath, sweat pouring from his skin, two certainties had arisen: one, the surprisingly strong surge of both excitement and protectiveness that he'd experienced for the tiny baby whose picture he now carried in his wallet, and two, the determination that he and Phoebe had much to work out.

She closed the menu, clearly decided on what she wanted to eat and smiled up at him. 'The gnocchi here is really good. It's my favourite.'

Shutting down the image of Phoebe coming to this restaurant with a date before jealousy stole what was left of his own appetite, Zach focused on using this opportunity to play catch-up, piecing together the facts he'd learned from Phoebe's conversation with Ali earlier. 'Have you had very bad morning sickness, then?'

He was glad to see that Phoebe's appetite had returned, but now that she was already into the second trimester of this pregnancy, he wanted to know what else he'd missed. Not only had he rushed out this afternoon and bought up every child-development and parenting book he could find, for some bizarre reason, he couldn't shake the feeling that he should have been there for Phoebe during those early weeks, not, from the way she'd resolutely maintained her stance on going it alone, that she'd have allowed it, no doubt.

Eyeing him warily again, as if she was suspicious of his motives, Phoebe sipped her water and shrugged. 'It's not too bad now. I usually make up for it by eating more for the rest of the day.'

'I'm glad that it's settling,' he said. Now that he'd raised the hot topic, Zach had many more questions, so she'd better get used to the idea. 'Are you taking pregnancy vitamins?'

'Of course.' She sat straighter as if offended. 'I'm doing everything I'm supposed to do. I've even given up my favourite: coffee. I just can't stomach it any more, even the smell.' She shuddered.

'I didn't mean to accuse you,' he said, as if he were traversing a path of eggshells. 'I just feel as if I've missed so much already. You should know by now that I like to stay informed.' He hadn't planned to become a father, but, now that it had happened, his head was full of dreams and fantasies of the future.

Phoebe's eyes widened. She looked startled by his admission.

'So there's no detox challenge at the hospital?' he asked, calling her out on her earlier excuse.

'No.' She glanced down, sheepishly. 'I panicked when you suggested coffee. I'm sorry about that.'

Zach clenched his jaw, trying to cling to his indignation given that she'd lied and then dismissed him, as if he had no investment in becoming a father. Except knowing that she was carrying his child, seeing her vulnerable after her dizzy spell, witnessing the unguarded moments of her interaction with her close friend and the way she'd been as awed as Zach by the ultrasound scan images had shown him new sides to Phoebe's personality that he couldn't help but find appealing.

More fool him.

Frustrated at his weakness for a woman who'd clearly stated that she was done with him more than once, he looked away from her profile as she placed her order with the server.

She was certainly testing the resolve he'd made to set his attraction aside so he could verbalise his feelings about the pregnancy and a way forward clearly. Every time she shifted in her seat or rested an elbow on the table, the neck of her blouse gaped, revealing a vee of creamy chest. But he had much bigger issues to raise than his ongoing fascination with her. Like how, when it came to the child they'd made together, she'd already written him out of the story.

Determined to clear the air now that he'd had a chance to come to terms with the news, Zach waited until they were alone once more and said,

'I handled things badly earlier. I think I was in shock, if I'm honest.'

Shocked was an understatement; more like poleaxed. The idea of becoming a father in six months' time when he wasn't even in a relationship with the baby's mother had sent his brain spinning. He was always careful with his sexual partners, always used protection, but no method of contraception was one hundred per cent reliable. Then, as the seconds passed, the shock had been replaced by wonder, awe, joy.

'I handled it badly too,' she said, looking genuinely regretful, catching him off guard. 'I was a bit shaken myself in the beginning, as you can imagine.' She swallowed and a fresh wave of empathy took hold of his usually analytical mind.

'When I knew you were coming to Sydney, I'd planned a whole speech for when you arrived,' she said, toying with her water glass. 'But then you showed up early and I bungled it. I'm really sorry about the way you found out, Zach.'

Because he wanted to reach across the table and take her hand, show her that he'd forgiven her almost immediately back in her office, Zach instead took a sip of mineral water, avoiding alcohol in solidarity with a teetotal Phoebe.

He watched her over the rim of his glass, saw her uncertainty and doubt. It wasn't every day she had to confront a man she barely knew with life-changing news, especially when they hadn't planned to see each other again and when they'd been careful. He could understand the awkwardness and amplified emotions of the situation, particularly on the back of an emergency in the OR and when she'd been feeling unwell.

'Well, I've had some time to think since this afternoon,' he said, trying to ignore the fact that every time she looked at him, he recalled the way she'd automatically reached for his arm while they'd waited for the scan to locate their baby's rapid heartbeat.

In that tense split second, despite her assertions of going it alone, she *had* needed his presence for comfort.

Why had that felt so good? Was it just the ingrained caring that was a part of his job? Or was it evidence that, despite how she'd assured him that he had no role in the pregnancy, he'd seen a way that he could be of use beyond his relationship with his baby?

Of course he had a role. A vital one, although she might not like the idea.

'I know you said that you don't need me,' he said, trying and failing to hold onto the brief flicker of anger he'd felt when she'd dismissed him earlier, 'which is totally your prerogative. But I think it's important that I be around, for both you and the baby.'

His baby.

She might not need him, but their baby needed its father as much as he needed to be a part of his child's life.

Phoebe gaped, disbelief written all over her heart-shaped face. 'You want to be involved?'

Zach nodded. 'Of course.' Just because he was no more interested in a relationship than she was, didn't mean that he couldn't support her through the rest of the pregnancy now that they were to be parents.

'But…your lifestyle,' she said, frowning, 'the way you travel. It's hardly suited to changing nappies and sleepless nights.'

Faced with her patronising comment, Zach bit back his first retort. He didn't want to upset her or even argue the point. She was right. He was forty-one and single. He'd certainly been around the block, had a healthy sex life, but he'd always avoided commitment. He couldn't see the point in investing all of that time and energy into a relationship when it was most likely doomed to failure, the way his parents' twenty-six-year marriage had ended.

Being trapped in the middle of his parents' bitter divorce as a teenager had given him a deep and lasting insight into the fickle transiency of love.

But this wasn't just about him and Phoebe any longer. There was their baby to consider.

'And your lifestyle *is* suited to a baby?' he said, pointing out how similar they were and taking no satisfaction from the flush that pinkened her cheeks.

She raised her chin, challenge shining from her stare. 'You're right—neither of us planned this. But as we saw from the scan, it's happening. And I'll figure out the logistics, rest assured.'

'Alone?' he asked, while she straightened her cutlery on the white linen tablecloth, avoiding his gaze.

'Yes, alone. Lots of people do,' she said, meeting his gaze with defiance, as if reiterating her independence. 'Just because I'm pregnant, doesn't mean that I've changed who I am as a person.'

'Of course not,' he said, wondering where her fierce self-reliance originated. 'But this is going to be a major adjustment for both of us. I'm an uncle, so I've witnessed how a child changes *everything.*'

Their lives would never be the same again. How could they? He'd seen his siblings' lives both exponentially enriched and, in some ways, turned inside out by parenthood, not that any of them would admit to the latter, given the competitive streak that ran through all of the Archer siblings.

'And although I don't exactly have all of the details worked out right now,' he continued, pointedly holding her gaze, 'I want you to know that I intend to have a role in my child's life.'

A full and active role.

She could be as independent as she pleased, but Zach wouldn't tolerate being superfluous as a father, better that she understood that from the start. He had as much right as she did to parent their child. 'You're right, Phoebe,' he continued, 'we didn't plan this, but we made this baby together. That means we need to find a way to parent our child together too.'

Even if they weren't a romantic couple.

She looked away, a ghost of a smirk around her mouth. 'Of course.'

'What does that look mean?' he asked, sensing her unspoken cynicism. 'Don't you believe that my intentions are sincere?'

Was she suggesting he'd lie, go back on his word, shirk his responsibility once the baby was born? That showed how little she knew him. Just because they weren't in a relationship didn't mean that he would abandon his child or Phoebe. They were doctors, acutely aware that pregnancy sometimes carried risks and complications, especially a geriatric pregnancy. Zach wanted to be around, not only for their baby's welfare, but also in case a complication arose.

For now, he'd keep that to himself. Clearly Phoebe had a pretty low opinion of him if she thought him capable of simply walking away from both her and the baby he already felt fiercely protective of.

'It's not that I disbelieve you,' she said, looking uncomfortable, as if cornered. 'I'm sure that you mean what you're saying right now.'

'But?' he asked, because he knew it was coming. 'You think I'll change my mind?'

'But a child is for life,' she said, condescendingly, as if this thought hadn't yet occurred to him, as if their baby were a puppy he wouldn't have time to walk or a brightly painted fridge that seemed like a good idea at first, but then grew tiresome. 'That's a long-term commitment.'

Zach offered her a tight smile. 'Are you suggesting that the novelty of being a father will wear off? Because you know from my reputation as a surgeon that I'm not a quitter.' Once set on a course of action he deemed best, Zach committed one hundred per cent. Being a father that his child could depend upon, loving his child unconditionally so their baby grew up emotionally secure was the only satisfactory course of action.

She met his stare, her eyes full of resolve and something else, maybe hurt, vulnerability. 'It happens.' She shrugged, obviously expecting him to fail.

But the more Phoebe pushed him away, doubted his abilities, set him up for failure, the more determined her insinuations made him to also prove her wrong in the process. Not only would they be finding a way to co-parent their child, but they'd also be getting to know one another personally, starting right now, so that he could challenge whatever prejudices she held and make sure she understood the real Zach Archer.

In the same way that he strived to be the best surgeon he could be, he'd also aim to be the best father any kid could have. Not that he knew the first thing about raising a child, but he'd make it work in the same way he tackled any new challenge: with drive, determination and gallons of self-belief.

She took a sip of water and added, 'I haven't seen my own father since I was four years old, when he walked out on me and my mother.'

Zach's jaw started to ache where his muscles were clenched hard. So this casual admission was the root of her pretty low opinion of him, her own father the yardstick she measured all fathers against.

'I'm sorry that happened to you,' he said, his voice softening with empathy. 'But just because some men walk away from their responsibilities, doesn't mean that *all* men will. This is my baby too.'

Rolling her shoulders back, she clasped her hands together in front of her as if, having shown him one tiny glimpse of vulnerability, she was once more blocking him out. 'I know that, and I think it's better for all three of us, you, me and the baby, if we keep things real, keep our promises and expectations pragmatic. You and I need to be honest with each other for the baby's sake.'

Nodding his agreement, Zach considered his next words carefully. She didn't trust him, that much was clear. A part of him couldn't blame her. This so-called father of hers had abandoned her and never returned. It stood to reason that she'd be cynical about the intentions of her own baby's father. But Zach wasn't that sort of man. He constantly held himself to the highest standards in everything he did. He would give his all to parenting this baby, a baby he'd never imagined but already loved with shocking ferocity.

Did every parent experience this overwhelming swell of emotion?

'I agree,' he said, leaning back in his chair to give Phoebe some emotional space. 'So I'll start right now. If I'm honest, it feels as if you'd rather that I wasn't part of the picture.' He kept his voice even, despite that itch of impotence flaring anew, galvanising him to fight his corner. She might not realise that she was doing it, but she'd begun pushing him away, even before she'd told him about the baby. Her expectations of him couldn't be any lower.

Watching her reaction, her expression turning from one of shock to one of defensiveness, he tried to relax his shoulders, aware that this situation, the lack of control, was pushing him so far out of his comfort zone he'd need a GPS to find his composure once this meal was over. Perhaps he could be a little more objective about her point of view if he weren't still enslaved by their chemistry.

'That's not true.' She shook her head, rejecting his claim, although she couldn't meet his stare. 'I'm just highly aware of the circumstances, that's all. We're not in a relationship. We have demanding jobs and yours takes you all over the world.' She looked at him then, her eyes hardening. 'Realistically, I'll be doing this alone, and I'm absolutely fine with that.'

Zach bit his tongue. He *did* travel a lot. But she was setting him up to fail at fatherhood even before the baby was born. Just because they'd only planned on a one-night stand, didn't mean he had no interest in the unforeseen consequences. Just because he was male didn't mean he should be measured against another man's shortcomings. Just because he wasn't the one carrying the baby, didn't mean that his feelings were any less relevant.

He *would* be a good father.

Failure wasn't in his vocabulary. That was why he avoided his large family's gatherings whenever possible, having, up until now, no interest in the competition to produce grandchildren for his parents, a race in which he'd always been automatically disqualified by default.

But things changed. People changed. Priorities changed.

For a second, he imagined telling his parents that their youngest son had finally produced their next grandchild. They were going to be overjoyed.

'I'm sorry that you have so little faith in me,' he said, taking the gauntlet that she'd so casually thrown down. 'But you and I are both similarly dedicated people. We like to do things to the best of our ability. I saw that today in the operating theatre. I plan on applying that same dedication to raising our child, as, I suspect, will you.'

Still suspicious, she eyed him non-committally.

'So, I have a proposition,' he added with a smile, embracing the challenge to show her how wrong she was about him, confident as always in his own abilities. 'I'm due in Perth in three weeks for a month-long visiting-surgeon post. How about we use the time I'm in Sydney to not only figure out a plan for when the baby arrives and for the future, but also get to know each other better? As you said—honesty is the best policy.'

That hadn't been the point of her speech, which had been to demonstrate her surety that he would behave just like her own father. But he and Phoebe understanding each other, learning the other's priorities, goals and values, could only be a good thing in the long run, especially for their baby.

'What do you say?' he asked, raising his glass. 'To getting to know each other and to co-parenting.'

Phoebe touched her water glass to his almost reluctantly, doubt lingering in her eyes. 'To getting to know each other.'

Determined to show her not only that he was a man of his word, but that he could also be trusted, he resolved to be patient.

But one thing was certain—if Phoebe thought she had everything neatly sorted, excluding him from his baby's life in the process, she'd grossly underestimated his single-mindedness.

CHAPTER SEVEN

LATER THAT WEEK, Phoebe walked into the neonatal intensive care unit, or NICU for short, where tiny newborn twins Poppy and Jasmine Wilson were inpatients, her stomach tight with nerves. She should be getting used to seeing Zach around Sydney Central by now, but the impending sight of him, after everything that had transpired that first day, was something she both looked forward to and dreaded.

She'd been utterly thrown by his assertions at dinner that first day. She'd never in a million years have imagined that he'd want to hang around, to be involved with the pregnancy and participate in raising the baby. She'd almost spluttered out her water when he'd proposed that they would not only be co-parenting, but also getting to know each other better and making plans for the future.

But he was still leaving in under three weeks, a fact that helped her to put his promises into perspective. Maybe, once he'd left Sydney, she and the baby would be a little easier to forget.

Phoebe turned the corner, her emotions all over the place once more. She spied Zach waiting at the desk, and her heart galloped. He was so handsome, so imposing and yet calmly confident. The way he'd steered the conversation at Tutto Bene, so self-assured that he'd figure out exactly how to be everything he needed to be—doctor, parent, platonic partner to the woman carrying his child—it was seriously impressive.

Of course, there were many hurdles ahead. Plenty of time for him to change his mind or mess up.

As she approached, she saw that Zach was chatting to one of the ward nurses, a pretty, bubbly redhead in her early thirties. Out of nowhere, white-hot jealousy pierced Phoebe's side like a stitch.

Of course Zach's charisma and self-possession naturally put people at ease, making him approachable and engaging. Not to mention the fact that he was the sexiest man Phoebe had ever known, something she just couldn't ignore, no matter how hard she tried. She'd already heard the whisperings around the hospital, tales of the new hottie neonatal surgeon with the sexy deep voice, dreamy eyes and yummy backside.

Resisting the urge to fan her flushed face, Phoebe interrupted. 'Dr Archer.'

She paused at his side and flashed both him and Nurse Maynard a smile. It meant nothing to her if Zach wanted to move on to his next casual conquest. Despite his reassurances that he intended to be there for her and the baby, she'd meant what she said. She didn't need him, nor did she have any intention of acting on her inescapable attraction to the man. They might be about to become parents, but that didn't mean that Phoebe needed a romantic relationship in order to be happy. Rosa Mason had seen to it that her only daughter would be raised to know her own worth and never rely on a man.

Rather than shaping his own destiny and taking care of his responsibilities, Phoebe's father had blamed Rosa for his disappointments in life. Phoebe only had one memory of the man, a vague blurry image of him pushing her on a merry-go-round, his smiling face looming in and out of focus with each revolution, distorted by her dizziness.

But there was more to being a father than donating sperm. As Phoebe had grown older, she'd stopped watching the door waiting for him to come back and take her to the park once more. Instead, she'd channelled all of her disappointment into being helpful to Rosa, who'd worked long, hard hours to be all the parent Phoebe had needed.

Thinking about her mum, she realised that now that she'd told Zach about the baby, she would no longer need to keep it a secret from her mum. They spoke most evenings on the phone, were very close. Or perhaps she'd wait until she had time to visit, tell her mum in person.

'Shall we?' she said to Zach, gesturing that he follow her to the side ward where the twins and Emma, their mother, were inpatients. Baby Jasmine, Poppy's twin, was growing stronger by the day, so Emma had once more been admitted in order to try and establish Jasmine on breast feeds alone prior to her discharge.

Pausing at the sinks outside the side ward, which afforded the high-profile family some privacy, Phoebe donned a surgical mask and washed her hands. Becoming aware of Zach's eyes on her as he mirrored her actions, she looked up.

'How are you feeling this morning?' he asked, his grey eyes soft and probing, as if she were made of glass.

'I'm fine,' she said, tugging some paper towels from the dispenser with unnecessary force, unused to anyone other than her friends asking after her well-being.

As if he doubted her automatic response, his gaze slowly and thoroughly roamed her features in that highly distracting way she recalled from that night in Brisbane when he'd made her feel like the only woman in the world.

'You still look a little pale,' he said, his voice low and intimate as he dried his own hands, stepping closer as if they were the only two people on the ward.

Phoebe stepped back, away from the tall, impressive wall of his body, from the heat he emanated and the memories of being clutched to his naked chest, clasped in those strong arms of his.

'I didn't sleep very well,' she said, defensive and aroused, a confusing mix that left her irritable. Did he intend to check in with her every morning in his quest to show her that he'd meant what he'd said about wanting to be involved? Did he disbelieve that she was taking all possible steps to ensure a healthy pregnancy? Surely delivering food and asking after her health was taking his paternal duties too far. They weren't a couple, so there was no need to shower Phoebe with such devoted consideration.

'I managed to finish my breakfast, so that's progress,' she said, because he was still staring, his attentiveness unsettling. She wasn't used to it and had no intention of growing dependent on his concern. It made her feel somehow incapable or beholden.

'Good.' He smiled, looking inordinately pleased,

as if she'd won a gold medal for muesli consumption. 'I'm glad.'

To her horror, Phoebe's hormone-ridden body actually preened, as if craving his praise. Well, that was enough of that.

'Emma Wilson,' she said, deciding to bring him up to speed on the ordeal the Wilson family had already been through these past three months since Emma was first admitted, 'is the mother of twins, Poppy and Jasmine, who were born by uncomplicated caesarean section performed by Ali Edwards, who you met.'

Zach nodded at her summary. 'Yes. I arrived early and read Poppy's and Jasmine's notes. I told you—I like to be prepared.'

Taken aback by his diligence and commitment, Phoebe blinked up at him. So far, everything she thought she'd known about Zach Archer was being systematically challenged. Despite his reputation for taking charge, he'd willingly acted as her assistant in Theatre these past few days. Rather than freak him out, as she might have guessed, her news that they were going to be parents hadn't sent him running. Instead, he'd declared they should get to know each other so they could act as an effective co-parenting team. And now, when he could easily have slept in to recover from his jet lag, he'd come in before eight in the morning to bring himself up to speed on Poppy Wilson's history.

'Okay, then,' Phoebe muttered, a little breathless, 'let's go meet the Wilsons.'

They entered the room to find the tall, dark and handsome Aaron Wilson alone with his daughters. The well-built man was sitting in an armchair holding a sleeping Jasmine in the crook of his muscular arm.

Aaron looked up from staring lovingly at his tiny daughter, who wore a pale yellow hand-knitted hat, one of hundreds a year that were donated to the unit by the volunteer knitters of Sydney. Smiling in welcome, Aaron explained that Emma was just dressing after a shower.

'Aaron, this is Dr Archer, the specialist I told you about,' Phoebe said, a flush of silly pride warming her chest, as if she had some sort of ownership of Zach.

But of course she didn't. Just because she still fancied the pants off him, didn't mean she'd changed her stance on relationships. And Zach hadn't said anything about them rekindling what they'd shared in Brisbane, so her hormones could forget it.

'Call me Zach,' Zach said, shaking Aaron's free hand. 'It's good to meet you. And this must be Jasmine.'

The two men talked for a few minutes about

Jasmine's progress, her weight gain and attempts at breastfeeding, Zach taking the lead on the consultation and leaving Phoebe free to simply watch him in action.

Zach had indeed thoroughly read the extensive notes on both twins, and even, it seemed, on Emma, the questions he asked relevant and insightful. This was what made him so good at his work. His meticulous attention to detail, his inexhaustible self-belief and his ability not only to take the initiative, but also to humbly relate to people in a way that instantly put them at ease.

A little awed by Zach, Phoebe listened while he explained that because both twins were so small and tired so rapidly, they were still being fed Emma's expressed breast milk by nasogastric tube. That Jasmine had been latching on for short periods of time overnight was a good sign that she might soon be ready for discharge.

Poppy, however, was a different matter.

Before they could move on to discuss Poppy's progress, Emma called for her husband from the adjoining bathroom. Aaron stood and moved to place Jasmine back in her crib, but Zach intervened.

'Here, allow me.' Without hesitation, Zach relieved Aaron of his tiny bundle, scooping an undisturbed Jasmine into his arms.

While Aaron left the room to help his wife,

Phoebe gaped, her heart pelting away with excitement behind her ribs. Rather than place Jasmine back in her crib, Zach held her with the same reverence that Aaron had displayed, glancing down at her as if she were the most fascinating thing he'd ever seen.

Phoebe froze, spellbound by the sight of Zach holding Jasmine's head in the palm of his capable surgeon's hand. He didn't coo or rock the baby, merely stared, his gaze taking in her sleeping form from head to toe.

Phoebe's stomach flipped over and over as reality rushed in, almost swiping her feet from under her. In the messy confusion and bungled announcement that their one passionate night had led to consequences—their own baby, in her rush to control her hormones and switch off her still rampant attraction to the man, in her insistence to show that she didn't need his help in parenting their child, she'd completely overlooked the fact that, as a world-leading neonatal surgeon, Zachary Archer had some serious baby-handling skills.

She swallowed, her throat dry. Just watching him in action with Jasmine, all six-foot-plus of him, unselfconsciously holding a baby, almost made her body spontaneously combust with lust.

His words that night in the restaurant hit her in the centre of her chest, more potent than the first time she'd heard them, when she'd managed to easily dismiss them as mere lip-service.

I intend to have a role in my child's life.

What if he truly meant it? What would that mean for Phoebe? Would she have to see him all the time, be constantly bombarded by lust?

No, even if he did plan to accompany her for blood tests and scans and deliver her lunch if she was too busy, he was leaving Sydney soon, although perhaps not soon enough...

She'd arrogantly misjudged Zach, assumed that he'd react in ways she'd imagined her father might have reacted from the tales her mother told. That didn't mean anything had changed. They still weren't a couple. And just because he didn't resent her for his altered circumstances at this moment, the way her father had blamed her mother before he'd walked out on them, didn't mean that he'd always feel that way. Maybe one day, when reality dawned, when fatigue set in, when perhaps the burden of parenthood became too heavy, he might blame Phoebe for disrupting his old life.

Who knew how those strains of worry and responsibility might affect the fragile, co-parenting relationship he seemed to think would be easy? No matter what assertions he'd made, the novelty of Sydney, of three a.m. feeds and sick-up stains on his expensive shirts would surely fade.

Getting to know each other beyond their well-established chemistry was one thing. Agreement, compromise and expectation were entirely different beasts. Neither of them had any experience of those things as far as long-term relationships were concerned.

As Phoebe tried to get her breathing under control, tried to put everything back into perspective, Zach carefully transferred a still-sleeping Jasmine to her crib. She looked away, because Zach holding a baby was ten times hotter than the Zach already stirring up her libido and confusing her with thoughtful gestures and enquiries, as if he cared about her as well as their baby.

Because her legs felt unsteady, she gripped the edge of Poppy's crib. She and Zach were going to be parents, just like Aaron and Emma.

Only unlike the Wilsons—a loving and committed couple—they'd be separate, alone.

Co-parenting. It had sounded progressive and neat when Zach had said it over dinner, but now she couldn't shake the feeling that it also sounded lonely. Seeing his gentle and nurturing side was bound to bring her doubts and fears to the surface. It gave her an insight into how he might parent their own child, a tantalising glimpse of how their child's life might differ from what her own had been.

Just then, Emma and Aaron emerged from the

bathroom, Emma still walking gingerly to protect her sutured abdominal incision, while Aaron lent her his arm for support.

Zach introduced himself to the twins' mother, offering a handshake and his signature charismatic smile that shunted Phoebe's body temperature a few degrees higher.

How dared he be so good at everything? No wonder she was all over the place again. Just when she thought she'd figured Zach out, he surprised her anew, like those impossible puzzle cubes, where one move undid each previous solution.

'So, I know it's been explained to you before,' Zach said, 'but I just wanted to go over the plan for Poppy's surgery one more time.' He clarified every detail of ventricular septal defect, an abnormal connection between the two main chambers of Poppy's heart, in a non-patronising way, drawing diagrams to illustrate the surgical procedure they would undertake to close the defect so that the direction of blood flow was corrected.

By the end of his explanation, Aaron and Emma seemed a little starstruck, just like Phoebe.

'So,' he continued, glancing Phoebe's way to include her in the conversation, 'while Poppy has the most common form of congenital heart defect, and while Dr Mason and I have done this type of surgery many times before, Poppy's prematurity, her low weight and the fact that she has been so resistant to our attempts to delay the operation, to treat her symptoms medically until she gains some more weight, make this surgery just a little more challenging.'

'That's why I brought in Dr Archer,' Phoebe said, conscious of the Wilsons' understandably concerned expressions. 'He's the best there is, so even though the defect in Poppy's heart is large, Zach and I have been over the scans and both feel happy with the surgical approach he's just outlined.'

'Why don't we examine Poppy, while you jot down any questions you might have?' Zach said, modestly breezing over Phoebe's compliment.

As Zach listened to Poppy's heart, Emma and Aaron held onto each other's hand tightly while they discussed the information and came up with their most immediate questions. Phoebe's respect for Zach had gone through the roof. He possessed just the right balance of optimism versus caution, outlining the potential risks of surgery in as compassionate and informative a way as possible. As Phoebe had met the family many times before, she could see that Aaron and Emma felt empowered by their good understanding of the surgery and of the complications of both proceeding with the operation, and waiting, as was the usual case in patients with VSD.

Removing his stethoscope from his ears, Zach held the bell in place over the front of Poppy's chest.

'Have a listen,' he said, handing the earpieces to Phoebe, who fitted them in place. With his hand, he gently positioned her hand and the bell of the stethoscope.

For a few seconds they stayed like that, Phoebe listening to the whoosh of Poppy's heart murmur, Zach holding her hand in place, his eyes locked with hers, silent communication passing between them.

He could have just been asking for her corroboration on the quality of the heart murmur so they could confer later. But the intimacy of the moment, the gravity of examining the unwell neonate together while their own baby grew safe and sound inside her, made Phoebe take a closer look at the type of man Zach was.

A complex man of integrity and professional dedication. A man of strong convictions.

Phoebe nodded to show him that she understood his unspoken message, doctor to doctor, parent to parent: their tiny patient, unlike her sister, was seriously unwell.

Phoebe repositioned the stethoscope over the base of Poppy's lungs, finding the faint crackle that indicated fluid build-up.

As he'd done, she passed the stethoscope earpieces back to him and replaced his hand with hers, this time guiding him to listen to the lung fields. The abnormal functioning of Poppy's heart was causing congestion in the lungs and other organs. The longer that went on, the greater the risk of irreversible organ damage. That was why the surgery couldn't be delayed any longer.

Wrapping up the examination, Zach covered Poppy with a blanket. They answered Aaron and Emma's questions honestly and with compassion they clearly shared. This family had been through so much, their inspiring strength arising from their loving relationship. Now that she and Zach were having a child of their own, Phoebe understood a fraction of the Wilsons' anguish and concern.

They left the room together, headed downstairs to Phoebe's office, Zach the first one to break the loaded and pensive silence.

'So Poppy is on the list for surgery early next week?' he asked.

Phoebe nodded, pushing through a set of double doors. 'Yes. I'll speak to the intensive care team, ask them to increase the inotropes and diuretics, see if we can optimise her lung function for surgery.'

Zach paused, touched her arm, bringing her to a halt, halfway down the stairs. 'I want you to know that, regardless of what's going on with us, personally, I'm glad you called me in on this case.'

Phoebe nodded, her burning eyes locked to his and her throat tight. 'I'm glad that you're here.'

She didn't need him, but she was grateful that he could assist on the surgery, his experience and intuition easing some of her concerns for Poppy and their shared secret bonding them in a way she couldn't have imagined when she invited him to Sydney.

She smiled and they set off once more. A strange empty feeling hollowed out her chest. They might be willing to tackle Poppy's case as a team, but could they tackle any future hurdles involving their own child as such? Would Zach even be around, as promised, to share the load? Or would she have to muddle through alone, the way her own mother had?

Just because he'd made some pretty ambitious declarations about being involved, didn't mean that she could rely on him to keep his word. People changed their minds, tended to their own needs, behaved selfishly. For as long as Zach was around, she'd need to take extra care to maintain her independence. No matter how much she struggled with their ongoing chemistry, no matter how good it felt to have him work temporarily at her side, emotionally, Phoebe could only truly rely on herself.

* * *

That Friday evening, a rare bout of nerves gripped Zach as he knocked on the closed door to Phoebe's office, the strength of which he probably hadn't experienced since his very first kiss.

Although he had spent day after day harmoniously working alongside her, Phoebe seemed to be the only woman alive who could tie him into convoluted knots. At work, they gelled, their complementary styles building on their mutual respect. But beyond professionally, there was a wall around Dr Mason that Zach just couldn't seem to scale.

They were going to be parents. He wanted the respect and cooperation they enjoyed at work to extend to their personal relationship, so, by the time the baby arrived, he and Phoebe operated as a team.

The door to her office swung open. 'Oh, hi.' Phoebe's face registered shock, but quickly turned to a hesitant smile. 'Did you need something?' she asked, adjusting the strap of her bag on her shoulder as if she was on her way home.

Perfect timing.

'I was hoping I could make you dinner.' Zach slung his hands casually into his trouser pockets while his heart pounded away nineteen to the dozen with those nerves, which made a mockery of his reputation for calm, unemotional decision-making. Now that she'd as good as written him off as a father, the pressure to prove himself trustworthy, to show her that he was a man she could rely on, was almost as overwhelming as the urge to seek out her company over and over again.

'I figured you might be tired after the busy week.' He stepped closer, relieved to see the flicker of interest in her unguarded stare, her rapid blinking matching the tempo of his pulse. 'It will give us a chance to talk, to get to know each other as we agreed.'

There was little time to talk about their personal lives at the hospital, what with surgery lists, clinics and ward rounds. On top of Phoebe's workload, Zach had also spent part of the week at the local clinic run by Nurture, seeing his own referrals.

Observing him with a fascination that left his body temperature a few degrees higher, Phoebe tilted her head. 'You cook?'

It shouldn't give him a kick of satisfaction to surprise her, but it did. And it also proved his point. They'd learned how to pleasure each other's bodies that night in Brisbane, they knew they could work together, but they still had so much to learn about the other's personality, passions and dreams.

'I do.' Zach nodded, his smile widening. 'Very well, in fact.'

Rolling her eyes, Phoebe teased, 'Of course you do—I'd expect nothing less. But aren't you staying at a hotel?'

Zach shook his head, confident now that he could win her over. 'I have an apartment here in Pacific Point.' The coastal suburb was a thirty-minute drive south of the city, his base whenever he was back in the country.

Phoebe raised her eyebrows, surprised and obviously impressed by his postcode. 'Um… I'd like nothing better than a home-cooked meal, but…'

'I'll take you home later,' he cajoled, part of him expecting another of Phoebe's quick and efficient brush-offs.

'It's not that. It's just that I was on my way home for a soak in the bath.' She gnawed at her lip, her cheeks flushing.

Trying not to think of Phoebe's naked, wet body, Zach kept the disappointment from his voice with effort. 'Perhaps another night, then.'

He stepped back to allow her room to pass, but had barely moved when she touched his arm. 'Unless… You could cook at my place, you know, while I take a bath.'

'I can cook anywhere there's a kitchen,' he said

with a grin, willing to do anything to spend another hour in her company.

She smiled, a vision that warmed his insides like a dram of whisky. 'Good. I live a ten-minute walk from the hospital. Although I have no idea what's in my fridge, but there's a mini-mart right next to my apartment if you need anything specific.'

Zach shrugged, relieved that she wanted both his company and his culinary skills. 'Good. Then it's all sorted.'

Zach held open the door and followed her along the corridor towards the exit. It was a small thing, but his steps were lighter now that she'd accepted his offer to cook. It felt like a tiny breakthrough in winning her trust.

Zach kept his satisfied smile to himself as they left the hospital and set off past the neighbouring office blocks, street-level shops and abundant cafés. The pavements were thick with commuters all heading for underground car parks, the train or the ferry, the atmosphere hindering intimate and meaningful conversation.

'So what can you cook?' Phoebe asked, amusement tugging at her mouth.

'I told you, I'm good. You name it and I can cook it.'

She laughed at his boast. 'So who taught you? An ex-girlfriend?'

Did he detect a hint of jealousy in her voice?

'I told you in Brisbane—there haven't really been many of those, especially not the serious kind.'

They paused at the intersection to wait for the lights to change. Phoebe looked up at him with curiosity.

'My parents taught me and my brothers and sister to cook,' he said, breaking the suspense. 'They worked long hours, sometimes shift work, so meal preparation was a team effort in the Archer household. I'm the youngest of four siblings, so after my siblings left home, I had plenty of time to hone my skills. I like food.' He tapped his flat stomach, rewarded by the way Phoebe's gaze swept over the body he kept in shape, appreciatively.

'What do you normally cook after work?' he asked, to gauge her likes and dislikes in order to come up with something quick, tasty and nutritious.

She offered him a sheepish smile. 'I live in central Sydney. I'm surrounded by cafés and restaurants. There's even an award-winning delicatessen on my street. I'm usually too busy to do more than a little reheating, maybe throw a salad together. There's no real point spending hours cooking for one person.' She shrugged and Zach nodded, wondering if she ever grew lonely.

Still haunted by the look of defeat on her face when she'd confessed to being deserted by her father, Zach resolved to understand what made her tick. On the surface she was self-possessed, competent, ambitious. But, like him, she'd never married. Had her father's abandonment given her a fear of commitment? It certainly explained her rather cynical opinion of Zach, one he hoped to change.

'I know what you mean,' he said, returning to the convenience of city living.

Their lives were similar: work, sleep, repeat. Busy lives that were only going to become busier once the baby arrived. But he had no doubt that he and Phoebe would make co-parenting work.

Of course he'd need to spend more time in Sydney if his baby was in Sydney.

'So any food dislikes, allergies or pregnancy aversions I should know about?' he asked as they crossed the road.

She shook her head, smiled. 'No. I like food too, and now that the morning sickness has pretty much stopped, I seem to be always hungry.'

'That's understandable,' he said. 'Your body is growing a whole new human being.' Now that it was happening to him, the miracle of pregnancy struck him in a way he'd previously taken for granted. Did Phoebe feel the same wonder?

Zach had watched Aaron Wilson hold Poppy's

sister, Jasmine, with envious fascination when they'd met earlier that week. Zach's own love for their child had hit him like a sledgehammer. The baby hadn't even arrived yet, but he already knew he'd do anything to defend and safeguard his child. But the real shock had come when the same feelings emerged whenever he thought about Phoebe.

Perhaps they could become friends, share the joys and trials of parenthood, be there for their child and each other.

Swallowing at how his fantasy sounded suspiciously like a relationship, Zach glanced at Phoebe.

'This is my building,' she said, pointing up at a mid-rise across the street as the lights changed.

They were about to step into the road when some idiot on an electric scooter whizzed past them from behind.

Phoebe yelped, ducking aside, colliding with Zach. His arm went around her waist automatically, his heart thumping as he glared after the inconsiderate commuter. Aware that he was clutching her in his arms for safekeeping, Zach glanced down. 'Are you okay? What an idiot,' he muttered. 'You could have been knocked to the ground.'

Protective urges flared along with the desire ransacking his anatomy. His arm flexed, bringing her closer as if of its own accord, bathing his senses in pure Phoebe—her subtle scent, the soft gust of her breath, her heart thudding against his chest.

'I'm okay,' she said, looking up at him with wide eyes. Only instead of seeing alarm or annoyance Zach detected reciprocal arousal.

So much for the fantasy of friendship. Friends didn't look at each other this way. Because he couldn't help himself, his gaze dipped to her parted lips, the urge to kiss her strong and instantaneous, like a primitive reflex.

But just because he'd kissed every inch of her body and made her cry out his name that night three months ago, just because she was looking up at him as if she wanted another night in his arms, didn't mean it was a good idea. In fact it could ruin his plan for a mature and considerate co-parenting team.

Flushing, Phoebe disentangled herself from his grip. Zach dragged in a breath, part of him wishing he *had* kissed her. But the moment was gone. They stepped back into the flow of pedestrians once more and made it to the entrance of Phoebe's apartment building in strained silence.

She keyed in a code and Zach followed her inside. Like a needle stuck in a scratch on a vinyl album, he kept returning to his physical attraction to the woman carrying their baby. His resolve to move past their sexual compatibility had been badly shaken by that thirty seconds of contact on the street, making the sensible and logical path he'd decided upon blurry and insubstantial like a wisp of smoke. He was right back where he'd started, craving Phoebe as much as he had that very first night they met, even though indulging those cravings could be disastrous.

Phoebe emerged from her bedroom, freshly bathed and dressed in her most comfortable track pants and sweater. The relaxing bubble bath had done nothing to calm the frantic, bone-melting excitement of stumbling into Zach's arms. But she couldn't hide in her own home, no matter how much she wished she could hide from the memory of his embrace, his searching expression as he'd gazed down at her, looking as if he might kiss her while their hearts thudded against each other. Drawn to the wonderful aromas coming from the kitchen, she padded hesitantly down the hall on bare feet, her insides a tangle of nervous anticipation.

Inviting him here had been a mistake. He was too tempting. At least at the hospital her inhibitions were contained by the fact that they were rarely alone.

Her stomach growled, but it was the sight of Zach in her small but well-equipped kitchen, his shirt sleeves rolled up, that made her mouth water. The strong, defined arms that had held her so tightly on the street, that had crushed her with such passion when they'd conceived their baby, were now gently whisking eggs in a bowl with the same skill he wielded a scalpel. Why was a man competent in the kitchen such a turn-on?

Or perhaps everything Zach did appealed to her.

'Whatever you're cooking smells amazing,' she said to cover the fact that her whole body shuddered as if desperate for more of his touch.

He looked up from the stove, his gaze meeting hers before taking an appreciative tour of her overheated body. 'I've made two of my quick and easy meal staples: Spanish omelette and three-ingredient chocolate mousse. Does that sound good?'

Phoebe nodded, swallowing hard at how easily she could grow used to having him in her home. 'Impressive. Is there no end to your talents?'

Silly question. Zach did everything to the best of his ability, be it the most intricate surgery or the simplest thoughtful gesture.

'Nope.' He winked and her breath caught. 'You should definitely share that opinion with my siblings when you meet them. We're a competitive bunch.'

Refusing to kill the mood by asking why and

when she was likely to meet Zach's family, Phoebe peered over his shoulder at a pan of simmering potatoes and another softening diced onion on the stove, noting how he'd not only skilfully manoeuvred his way around her kitchen, but also managed to connect his phone to her speaker and stream some chilled atmospheric music so this felt like a date.

'Can I do anything?' She watched him remove the cubes of potato from the water with a slotted spoon and add them to the onion.

His every move seemed to brush her sensitised skin, his relaxed stare making her feel exposed and…needy, as if getting to know his personal side made their chemistry harder and harder to fight.

'You could lay the table. I wasn't sure where to find place mats.'

To save herself from answering why she was fighting her attraction so hard, Phoebe laid the table in the adjoining dining area, setting two places side by side rather than the usual lonely one so they could both enjoy the distant harbour view overlooking her small balcony.

'Want a drink?' she said, opening the fridge and taking out a bottle of sparkling mineral water.

'Sounds good.'

She stood on tiptoes, reached overhead to retrieve two glasses from the cabinet above the stove. She must have imagined the small, strangled sound he made, because when she glanced his way he was adding the whisked eggs to the sizzling-hot pan.

Their chemistry was obviously mutual, but unlike in Brisbane, when their flirtation had been fun and finite, things were now more complicated. They had to work together. They were supposed to be building their relationship as parents.

If only her hormones weren't so persistent, reminding her how good they'd been together and how Zach would be leaving again in a couple of weeks anyway.

'So what do these highly competitive siblings do?' she asked, perching on the bench next to him, so she could indulge her curiosity and at the same time watch him cook.

'Jacob is a lawyer,' he said, dividing dark, glossy chocolate mousse between the small glass bowls she'd never once used. Normally she'd be trying to inhale the rich chocolate aroma, but all she wanted to do was nuzzle Zach's neck and inhale the delicious scent of his aftershave.

'Will runs his own successful export business,' he continued, placing the bowls of mousse in the fridge. 'And Janet, my sister, is head of Fly Media. They own Channel Ten and Matinee, the streaming service.'

Phoebe raised her eyebrows. 'Wow—what an inspiring family. Hopefully you've passed on some pretty smart genes to our baby.'

The thought of their child taking after Zach warmed her chest. Would she think of him every time she looked at their child, every time he or she said something smart or acted with kindness?

'I think our baby will also get those from you,' he said, licking a smear of chocolate from his thumb in a way that made Phoebe wish she could do the same.

Fortunately the distracting sight prevented her from wondering if she would miss him and their easy connection once he'd gone.

'My family is over-the-top competitive,' he said, with a wince. 'I hope *that* doesn't get passed on.'

Still hot and flustered from the remembered taste of his skin, Phoebe looked away from his sensual mouth, which had kissed her in every way possible: a soft tease, demanding and passionate, slow and seductive...

Stop thinking about kissing.

'So it's not healthy competition, then?' she said, taking a sip of ice-cold water, hoping to extinguish some of the heat coursing through her veins.

Zach shook his head, focused on finishing the omelette. 'Not if you call constant one-upmanship healthy, but it's kind of how we were raised. My parents are the children of Nigerian immigrants to Britain. They themselves emigrated to Australia from London when I was young. They weren't particularly well off, but they inherited a strong work ethic and encouraged all four of us to strive, to aim as high as we could in our chosen careers.'

'I'd say you've all made them proud by the sounds of it.' She didn't know his siblings, but Zach was a great guy, the whole package—caring, hard-working, talented.

'Oh, they are proud,' Zach said, turning off the heat and serving the omelette onto two plates. 'But family gatherings are pretty unbearable, with everyone trying to outshine each other. Who owns the biggest house or the best car? Whose wedding was the most extravagant and who has the most adorable children?' He shot her a quick glance. 'Not that I've entered myself into that particular competition, until now, but I think our baby will win, hands down, don't you?'

Phoebe froze, a lump stuck in her throat that Zach had already thought about their baby being cute. His intense eye contact was both playful and vulnerable in a way that made her want to reach out and cup his face, stroke her thumb over his cheekbone, tug him forward for the kiss she just couldn't scrub from her mind. What else had he imagined about the baby? Was he excited to meet their child, like her? Did she really want to know or was it better to hold back from sharing their dreams and hopes, given that he'd soon be leaving with no plan that she was aware of to return?

'Definitely,' she murmured, sliding from the bench and backing away from the moment of emotional intimacy.

'Dinner's ready,' he said, carrying the plates to the dining table, where she joined him with their glasses of water.

'So all your family lives in Sydney?' she asked as Zach placed her omelette in front of her. As he took a seat at her side her appetite for food disappeared.

How was she supposed to eat with him this close?

Zach nodded. 'They do, but my parents are divorced and deliberately live on opposite sides of the city, as far away from each other as possible.'

'So how many nieces and nephews do you have?' He probably knew more about kids than Phoebe did.

His fork hovered over his plate, his gaze dipping to her stomach, his eyes softening. 'Our baby already has seven cousins on my side.'

Our baby...

'Seven cousins...' She gasped, a little overwhelmed by the size of the extended Archer family, now their child's family too. While she'd been daydreaming about which of Zach's looks and personality attributes the baby would inherit, she'd overlooked the fact that he or she would also inherit a crowd of relatives on the Archer side.

She stared at Zach, unable to look away from his expression, which displayed the same hope and excitement she experienced every time she imagined finally meeting the tiny person growing inside her.

Compassion welled up in her chest. Of course Zach would feel the same connection to his unborn child. He'd love it as fiercely as Phoebe, was perhaps already falling in love with their growing baby.

Why was she only now considering the full implications of Zach wanting to be involved in their child's life?

'What about your family?' he asked, as if he hadn't noticed her sudden flare of panic at the enormity and complexity of their unorthodox situation. 'You mentioned your father…'

Phoebe shook her head. 'Talking about him is only going to take ten seconds. He married Mum, they had me and then he claimed he felt trapped.' She made finger quotes to highlight her poor excuse for a father's justification for doing a runner. 'For as far back as I can remember, it's always been just me and Mum,' she said, pushing the delicious-smelling eggs around her plate. 'I'm an only child, so we're very close.'

'What does your mother do?' he asked, his gaze searching as if he could see Phoebe's doubts and insecurities rising to the surface. But she'd long ago stopped wondering about the selfish man who'd donated half her genes.

Her worth was in no way reflected by the actions of a man like that.

'She's a community midwife in rural Queensland,' she said, smiling because, unlike her father, her mum was a force of nature.

He smiled. 'That's handy.'

Phoebe laughed. 'I'm hoping to persuade her to move to Sydney when she retires next year.' She took a bite of omelette, groaning when the sublime, perfectly balanced flavours hit her taste buds, although now that she'd realised the full implications of Zach being a part of her and the baby's life, now that she was more confused than ever about her attraction to him, she doubted that she'd be able to finish half of what was on her plate.

'I'm sure the lure of her grandchild will help. Is she excited about the baby?' Zach asked, watching her eat with a satisfied smile on his face.

Phoebe looked down, unsettled. 'I um…haven't

told her yet. I'm visiting home soon, thought I'd keep it a surprise, tell her in person.'

She couldn't confess that there was a tiny part of her that feared her mum's disappointment. Rosa knew exactly how hard it was to raise a child alone without any emotional or financial support from its father. She wouldn't want the same for Phoebe.

A small frown tugged Zach's mouth. 'So you don't have any other family here in Sydney? No one to help you with the baby?'

His question left her irrationally defensive. 'I have my amazing girlfriends, who I'm sure will help out if I need it. You met Ali. Harper heads up Sydney Central ER and Ivy is Head of General Surgery.'

'Are they happy for you?' Zach asked, inadvertently poking at another of Phoebe's soft spots.

'I haven't told Harper and Ivy my news yet, although I won't be able to hide it for much longer.' She automatically rested her hand on her belly. 'What about you? Have you told anyone?'

As soon as Phoebe told her friends, her mother, they would naturally ask who the father was. Until she'd told Zach, she hadn't been prepared for that question, but now she realised that she'd need to have an answer at the ready.

Catching Phoebe off guard, Zach slid his wallet from his pocket and took out the scan photo

Ali had given him. 'I'm going to tell my parents soon, separately of course, break the news that they're going to be grandparents again.' He smiled, sliding the grainy photo onto the table between them. 'I was wondering if you'd mind me showing them this.'

Phoebe stared at the photo, aware of Zach doing the same at her side. The urge to reach for his hand, to rest her head on his shoulder and whisper *Look what we made* was almost too strong to fight.

'Of course I don't mind,' Phoebe whispered, looking into his eyes. 'What happened with them?'

Was his parents' divorce the reason he avoided commitment?

Zach sighed, leaning back in his chair. 'They grew apart, finally divorcing when I was seventeen.' He shrugged, but nothing was ever that simple.

'After four children?' she asked, trying to understand the family dynamics. To understand Zach, who must have been more affected than he wanted to admit.

He scoffed. 'I know, right? They loved each other once, but now they can't be in the same room.'

'That must make things hard for you and your siblings.'

He nodded. 'It's exhausting, like crossing a minefield. We don't mention one parent in front of the other. At celebration times we're tugged in two different directions. Although, as the youngest, I copped the worst of being trapped in the middle after my siblings had all left home.'

Phoebe's heart thudded behind her ribs. No wonder he stayed single, preferring to focus on something with guaranteed success—his work.

'That must have been hard, Zach. I'm sorry.' Empathy squeezed her lungs, making it hard to breathe.

He cleared his throat and straightened in his chair. 'My time as piggy in the middle certainly gave me a unique insight. I would never inflict the heartache and uncertainty of a messy divorce on my child.'

As they finished their dinner, Phoebe marvelled at how much they had in common when it came to their views on relationships, their pasts, their families. The more she learned about the father of her baby, the harder it was becoming to resist their chemistry. Until Zach left Sydney she would need to take extra care to keep her distance, because what she absolutely couldn't do was allow feelings to cloud their already complex situation.

CHAPTER EIGHT

'THIS IS LITERALLY the best thing I've ever tasted,' Phoebe gushed, licking the spoon and then her lips after the first spoonful of chocolate mousse.

Zach looked away, pretending to find the view of the city from her small balcony fascinating, a long groan of frustration sounding in his head. If he'd thought her sexy little moan of delight at her first bite of the tortilla earlier had been bad enough to make him sweat, watching her lick the dark chocolate mousse from the spoon, her eyes closed in bliss, was enough to put him in a premature grave. She was literally killing him, the two-seater outdoor sofa that they shared making any sort of distance from temptation impossible.

'Glad you like it,' he croaked to stop himself from asking if he could taste it from her lips. The suggestion that they abandon the chocolate mousse for a different, more satisfying type of dessert lingered on the tip of his tongue.

What was he thinking? And why was he torturing himself this way?

Because aside from how much he still wanted her physically, he couldn't help but be drawn to her as a person, the future mother of his child, a kind and intelligent woman who, despite the example set by her absent father, had learned strength from her strong mother. Afflicted anew by the protective urges he just couldn't seem to switch off where Phoebe was concerned, he pondered why it gave him such satisfaction to cook for her. Yes, he applied his perfectionist tendencies to cooking, another thing at which he could excel. But it was more than just bragging rights. That she'd invited him to her home and given him the use of her kitchen, that she'd talked about her father and probed him about his family, made him feel as if slowly but surely, piece by piece, he could eventually win her trust. A prize worth striving for.

'So, have you thought about baby names?' he asked, hoping that her guard was sufficiently lowered to talk about the future.

She turned to face him, surprised by his question. 'Um, no. I guess I should give that some thought and you should too. We can swap notes and come up with a shortlist.'

Zach nodded, enjoying Phoebe's relaxed company and the excitement in her eyes whenever they discussed the baby. 'Just to warn you, as soon as I tell my mother about the baby, she'll start knitting a mountain of baby clothes, as she has done for her other grandchildren.'

Phoebe's eyes lit up as she licked another spoonful of mousse from the spoon.

'You don't have to use them if you don't like them,' he reassured her. Perhaps he should introduce Phoebe to his parents before he left Sydney. They were no longer a couple, but they would embrace and love this grandchild and Phoebe the way they had his siblings' children and partners. Perhaps it would be good for Phoebe to have a local family contact for those times when he was away? It would certainly ease his mind to know that she had some family close by.

'Oh, that's wonderful,' she said, genuinely delighted. 'My mother can't knit, so it will be all gratefully received.'

As he thought about his work commitments, being away from Sydney, from Phoebe and the baby, Zach's stomach churned. How would he make his job and fatherhood work? He certainly wouldn't tolerate doing the two things in a half-hearted fashion. But could he just move permanently back to Sydney? Phoebe had made it quite clear on multiple occasions that she was happy to go it alone.

But what did *he* want?

Taking another spoonful of mousse, she eyed him thoughtfully. 'Do you want to know the sex of the baby?' She glanced away, her voice growing quieter. 'I'll be happy to email you a copy of my next scan.'

Zach hesitated, his chest tight. Until he heard where Nurture might need him next, he wasn't sure where he'd be by the time of Phoebe's next scan, but it wouldn't be Sydney.

Could he truly tolerate being anywhere else while Phoebe was here alone, working full-time, struggling with fatigue with no one to help out, giving birth to his baby, alone? From her breezy, unemotional enquiry it was clear that Phoebe expected him to be absent, whereas he knew from the hollowness inside how much he would hate missing out on that next scan, or any other development in the pregnancy.

No one could be in two places at once. He'd have to make a choice, something that, until he'd met Phoebe, he had always found straightforward.

'Do *you* want to know the baby's sex?' Zach asked, his pulse thrumming in his throat at the intimacy of the turn in this conversation and how much closer he felt towards Phoebe.

'I'm not sure,' she whispered, as if caught up in the same spellbinding emotions and dawning realisations as Zach.

They were going to be parents, he and this woman he constantly wanted to be around. When he'd agreed to come back to Sydney for Poppy's surgery at Phoebe's request, he hadn't anticipated their growing emotional intimacy, nor had he imagined that he would want her so badly he could barely breathe.

'Well,' he said in a quiet voice, brushing a strand of hair away from her cheek, mesmerised by the way her stare clung to his, 'I think, as you're the one doing all the work at the moment, and you're the one who'll have to go through the birth, knowing the sex or not should be your choice. All I really want is a healthy baby, safely delivered and that you're okay.'

Of course he wanted the best for her, the best for their baby. But the idea of Phoebe in pain gave him chills. What if she needed him and he was overseas? What if he planned to be back in Sydney for the birth but the baby came early? It happened all the time. And why was he suddenly desperate to move whatever mountain necessary to be there for Phoebe for all of it?

Zach dropped his hand onto the back of the sofa to stop himself from touching her face. Until he figured everything out, it was best not to make promises he wasn't certain he could keep. He'd already done a complete mental flip tonight, initially convinced they needed to be a platonic team and then certain the best thing was to get all this sexual chemistry out of their systems.

'I think your brothers and sister should be worried,' she said, her voice low, her stare flicking between his eyes. 'You might give them a run for their money with the fatherhood thing.'

Zach swallowed. 'You think so?'

Phoebe nodded, her eyes shining.

He was too choked by her faith to gloat. Until a week ago, he'd never given much thought to being a father, but from the minute he'd seen that scan, heard the rapidly fluttering heartbeat of their baby, he'd wanted the best of everything for his and Phoebe's child.

'If I do decide to find out if it's a boy or a girl,' she said, her gaze dipping to his mouth in a distracting way that made him recall that moment on the street, when he'd almost kissed her, 'I'll let you know.'

'Okay,' he said, the urge to lean over and kiss her now almost overwhelming. Perhaps he should. Perhaps if they slept together again they could move on, focus on the plan to make co-parenting a success for the future.

Or it could ruin their chance at amicably raising their child together apart and make an already delicate connection much more complicated.

With the last hint of chocolate dying on her tongue, Phoebe placed her empty bowl next to

Zach's on the table, her pulse flying. 'That was delicious. Thanks, Zach.'

He was still staring at her as if he was poised to pounce. But maybe it was her imagination fuelled by hormones.

Except Zach had barely touched his own dessert while they'd talked about the baby. But he'd watched her eat hers, his eyes following the spoon to her mouth as if he wanted a taste from the same spoon, or from her lips.

Because he was still silent, because the chocolate, the hormones, Zach's proximity and their growing closeness had all conspired to make her unbelievably aroused, she filled the conversational gap with nervous chatter.

'The pregnancy hormones have given me terrible chocolate cravings,' she explained, brushing a speck of lint from her trouser leg, thinking of the violent mood swings and mental gymnastics she'd experienced since he'd arrived in Sydney. 'Perhaps because chocolate helps with the random bouts of inexplicable tears.'

She chuckled but Zach just stared, his head tilting as if in empathy.

She'd almost cried at least twice during the meal, once when she'd tried to visualise seventeen-year-old Zach trapped in the middle of his parents' divorce and again when he'd carefully tucked their baby's scan photo back into his wallet with as much care and tenderness as he'd used when he held newborn babies.

Why wasn't he saying anything?

'—although sadly, chocolate doesn't seem to help with the hormonal fluctuations,' she blabbered on. 'No one talks about that particular pregnancy side effect. I am constantly horn— Oh!'

She stopped talking, her face flaming as she realised that she was over-sharing, confessing intimate details of her overactive libido to the sexiest man alive, a man she knew could cure all of her pent-up frustration.

'Sorry, I forgot that you're not one of my girlfriends.' She fanned her face, embarrassed.

'Don't apologise,' he said, his voice gruff and his pupils dilated. 'We said we'd be honest. You can tell me anything, Phoebe.'

'Can I?' She stared, lost in his stare, a victim of the undeniable sexual tension that had ensnared her since the minute Zach had walked into the OR that first day.

He nodded, watching her lips as if waiting for a confession. But was it wise to raise the subject of the chemistry they were clearly both trying to ignore, to admit that she still wanted him as badly as the night of her birthday, perhaps even more, to suggest that they resume their fling for what time he had left in Sydney?

Exhaling a shaky breath, she stopped fighting. 'Because I'd have to tell you that I can't stop thinking about that incredible night in Brisbane.'

She might have imagined his groan; it was so low. 'Only if I can tell you I can't either.'

Light-headed, she held his stare, knowing that they were playing with fire, that she might open a door that might be difficult to close when the time came for Zach to leave. 'I still want you,' she whispered, 'but I'm scared to complicate things. We have to think about what's best for the baby.'

One night with Zach hadn't been enough to quench their chemistry, which was dangerous, intoxicating, nuclear-reactor hot.

As if he'd been waiting for permission, Zach reached for her hand where it rested in her lap. His strong, warm fingers gripped hers, his thumb stroking her knuckles in a soothing way.

'Thank you for your honesty. I agree, we'd need to be careful. To put the baby first.' His gaze flicked over her face, ending on her mouth. He wanted to kiss her.

She nodded, licking her lips, tasting the remnants of his dessert. Her head swam from the rush of his words and the heady possibilities.

'What do you want?' Her voice was husky with need. She trusted him with her body, but there was no room for feelings, which could only get in the way.

He leaned closer, cupped her face. 'I want you. But I don't want to hurt you.'

As if a fuse had been lit, the tingling sensation of his touch detonated in her chest, flooding her already needy body with heat. With a sigh of release, liberated by their honesty, she tilted her face up to his, their lips now only a whisper apart.

'I won't let you,' she said, transfixed by his lips, which were saying all the right things, which could deliver on their promise of pleasure. 'Think of it as a temporary fling to help me with my hormonal cravings, the way you've satisfied my chocolate cravings tonight.'

She smiled, tired of hiding how he made her feel.

He was leaving in a couple of weeks. Neither of them would risk feelings creeping in. They were too alike in their desire to avoid romantic complications. They could embrace a physical fling and then part amicably.

Once the baby arrived, she'd have no time for anything beyond juggling the demands of work and parenthood.

With a groan, his face grim with an almost pained expression, Zach's fingers flexed at the nape of her neck drawing her closer. His lips covered hers, hard, desperate. She clung to him, kissing him back, parting her lips to welcome the touch of his tongue to hers. He tasted like chocolate, rich and decadent. She moaned, gripping his shoulders, curling her nails into his flesh.

He pressed her back against the sofa, his powerful body surrounding her, holding her, matching her passion. She spread her legs, bucked her hips, seeking out the friction she craved before she actually combusted.

He pulled back, stared down at her, his eyes smoky with desire and his breath gusting. 'I've wanted to do that since that first day in Theatre.'

'Me too.' She nodded, her hands fisting his shirt, sliding underneath to caress the smooth skin of his muscular back as he swooped in and kissed a path along her neck.

His hand stroked her thigh, raised it over his hip so he could pin her back against the sofa with his hips, rocking into her, driving her wild.

'Zach... I want you,' she moaned, her body awash with tingles of desire. He was hard between her legs. She dropped her head back, exposed her neck to his kisses, granting him access to all of the places that made her toes curl with delight now that she'd finally surrendered to her desires.

Zach cupped her breast through her T-shirt, drawing out a whimper from her throat. If they didn't move to the bedroom soon, she'd have to start begging.

But no sooner had his palm cupped her sensitive flesh, coaxed the nipple erect, than he stopped, pulled back, dropped his hands to her waist and rested his forehead against hers, breathing hard.

'What's wrong?' she whispered, dazed, her hand resting over his galloping heart.

He knelt back so she could see his expression in the dark. 'We need to stop. I got carried away.'

'Why do we need to stop?' she asked, confusion making her voice whiny. 'Have you changed your mind?' She held her breath, praying he was still on board with the fling idea.

He stared, his gaze intense while indecision flitted over his expression 'No, absolutely not.' He dragged in a ragged breath, gripped the back of his neck, composing himself. 'It's just that you were tired when we left work and we have an early start tomorrow. You need your rest.'

'Oh… Of course. You're right.' Disappointment was rock in her stomach. Wishing that he weren't so noble, Phoebe nodded, tugging her sweater down and sitting on the edge of the sofa while she toyed with the idea of luring him to the dark side.

'We'll take a rain check, okay?' As if his mind was made up, Zach sat beside her, a determined set to his mouth. He put his arm around her shoulders and pressed a chaste kiss to the top of her head while their rapid breathing normalised.

'Absolutely.' She rested her head against his shoulder so she could sniff his neck in consolation.

How dared he be so honourable? But now that he'd mentioned it, she was tired.

After a few minutes, Zach stood, held out his hand and pulled her to her feet. Tilting up her chin, he pressed a kiss to her lips, his eyes still harbouring a hint of lingering arousal.

Inside the dark apartment, he grabbed his coat. 'There are leftovers in the fridge in case you can't be bothered to cook tomorrow.'

They moved to the hallway and opened the front door, the look he shot her full of regret. 'I hope you manage to get a good night's sleep.'

'Thanks for cooking dinner,' she said, scared she might actually drag him back inside and hold him hostage for the night.

He crossed over the threshold, almost reluctantly.

Phoebe gripped his arm, stood on tiptoes and kissed him once more, a proper goodbye that she could tell almost turned the tide on Zach's highly impressive resolve.

'That's for the chocolate mousse,' she said, desire turning her voice husky. She wasn't playing fair, but she wanted to leave him with an appetiser for next time.

Who knew when *next time* would be with their busy schedules?

Looking gratifyingly torn, Zach kissed the tip of his finger and pressed it to her lips. 'I have plenty more chocolate recipes to help with those cravings.'

'I look forward to it,' she said, aware that she might come across as a lust-struck teenager if she didn't release him soon.

He dragged in a deep ragged breath that told her he was struggling to leave as much as she was struggling to let him go.

She stepped back inside the apartment. 'Goodnight, Zach.'

'Goodnight, Phoebe.' His gaze swept down her body one last time, lingering for a second on her stomach. 'Goodnight, baby,' he whispered, meeting her stare once more.

His eyes were full of promises. The ones that left her wishing away the unknown length of time until they could be together again were welcome. The ones that accompanied his words to their unborn child she didn't dare believe.

This time, the third time that evening, she surrendered to the bout of hormonal and fatigue-induced tears, but only once she'd closed the door and was alone.

CHAPTER NINE

A FEW DAYS later there was a collective breath-hold in Theatre Three as the cardiopulmonary bypass machine was weaned off in preparation for leaving Poppy's newly repaired heart and tiny lungs unsupported.

Zach locked eyes with Phoebe across the operating table. Her emotions were easily identified in her eyes, the only part of her face visible over the top of her surgical mask. Hope that they'd done their job, that when Poppy's heart was restarted, the repair would hold. Comfort from the way they'd supported each other during the surgery, effectively working as a team. And the hardest thing to witness: a hint of fear.

Zach normally left his feelings at the door when he was operating but working together intuitively with Phoebe to repair Poppy's heart had amplified every emotion he'd been experiencing since that night at her apartment, when they'd opened up about their pasts, talked about their baby and then kissed.

Zach gave Phoebe a small nod of encouragement, showing her that he too felt all of her concerns. The fear for Poppy was real. The surgery to fix the large defect in the heart wall had been technically difficult and long. But where every surgery was important, the stakes on this one seemed greater, perhaps because Zach and Phoebe carried the secret knowledge of their own child. They could empathise with the Wilson family in a deeply personal way.

'Normothermia achieved,' the anaesthetist said as Poppy's core body temperature reached thirty-six degrees.

Phoebe blinked, her gaze not wavering from Zach's as they silently communicated.

This was the moment of truth.

The time had come to restart Poppy's heart and hope that the surgical repair was sound. Like Phoebe, he'd performed this surgery many times before. But Poppy's fragile condition, her low weight and prematurity added to the risks and therefore to the degree of clinical concern.

'Blood gasses look good,' the anaesthetist said. 'Adding inotropic support now.'

Phoebe's mask moved. Zach wondered if she was chewing her lip in a nervous gesture. Their growing emotional connection, the way she'd started opening up to him, showing him glimpses of her vulnerable side, had him questioning everything he thought he knew about himself, about his work, about the kind of life that had previously given him contentment. If they weren't sterile and in the middle of a surgery, he'd reach out and take her hand for her comfort and for his own.

At the nod from the anaesthetist, Phoebe removed the clamps from the major vessels to and from Poppy's heart. For a few tense seconds as the organ filled with blood, she and Zach stared, willing the heart to beat of its own accord. Zach was about to reach for the defibrillator paddles, when there was a brief flickering of the cardiac muscle, and the heart began beating a regular rhythm, which was picked up by the monitor, the sound amplified throughout the OR like a triumphant fanfare.

An audible collective sigh of relief passed around the room.

Zach grinned under his mask, his stare hopefully conveying his admiration to Phoebe. 'Well done,' he said in a low voice, a sense of pride and togetherness warming his blood. They'd done it, worked as a team, operated together on this tiny vulnerable baby girl, for whom the immediate signs were promising.

'We have sinus rhythm,' Phoebe said, slowly exhaling, like Zach, fighting for composure.

Zach wanted to hold her so badly, it almost

killed him to stay professional. The surgery wasn't complete—Poppy needed them still.

Phoebe dragged in a long breath. 'Thanks for your assistance,' she said, her stare lingering on his as if she had so much more she wanted to say. 'Let's check for leaks and repeat the echo.'

Zach nodded, checking the integrity of the atrial sutures for signs of leakage. As if he'd been postponing thinking about it until Poppy was out of danger, reality rushed his mind.

He and Phoebe wouldn't be working as a team for ever. He'd soon be leaving Sydney, leaving her and the baby behind.

How could he justify his absence given the new and delicate closeness between him and Phoebe? Perhaps he could finish up his current commitments in Perth and relocate to Sydney permanently... He'd be on hand to help out with the baby when Phoebe needed him. His child would grow up spending equal amounts of time with both parents. He and Phoebe could continue to work on their relationship, which would be vital for everyone's happiness in making their complex situation work.

But what would Phoebe think of his idea?

Focusing once more on the job in hand, they repeated the transoesophageal echo scan to ensure the synthetic patch was working and the blood flow through Poppy's heart was normalised before proceeding with the final stage of the operation.

'Everything looks good,' he said to Phoebe, directing the suction to the small collection of fluid around Poppy's heart. Phoebe nodded and began to suture closed the pericardium, the sac around the heart.

Zach assisted by stitching the drains into place. A growing sense of harmony gripped him, as if Phoebe's success was his success, and vice versa, where he'd previously considered himself a bit of a lone wolf. Self-sufficient. Complete.

As he watched Phoebe work, knowing that this beautiful, smart and dedicated woman would soon be the mother to his child, the alien yearning feeling in his chest that he'd awoken with for the past two mornings intensified. The closeness he felt towards her went beyond physical attraction.

For him, the baby gave them a shared bond that felt unshakable in a way he'd never before imagined he would experience. Now that he'd come to terms with the fact he was going to be a father, he wanted to explore the future with Phoebe, to discuss everything from baby names to preschools. To figure out their respective parenting styles and brainstorm the likely hurdles, the ups and downs so they could prepare for anything.

But that had always been Zach's way: identify

an issue and work to find a solution, not that their baby was an issue, more like a wondrous gift.

Snapping him from his thoughts, Phoebe said, 'I'm happy to close up here, Dr Archer, if you want to finish for the day.'

She kept her head down, her stare focused on closing the chest, the operation almost complete.

'Um, of course.' He stepped away from the table, trying not to feel dismissed now that she no longer needed his assistance. 'Would you like me to speak to Poppy's parents, let them know that the surgery has been successfully completed?' He peeled off his gloves and tossed them into the bin.

'Yes, please,' she said, casting him a quick cursory glance.

He knew what it was like to be *in the zone* while operating. But for a few minutes, he'd felt so emotionally in tune with her, been so carried away with his daydreams for their child, that he'd almost forgotten that Phoebe cherished her independence. That Sydney Central was *her* turf. That she might not welcome him living and working on her doorstep.

'Tell them I'll be along shortly to speak to them also,' she added, 'once Poppy is back on NICU.'

'Sure.' Zach hesitated, struggling to separate the tangle of feelings today—a long and tense day—had unearthed.

But now he recalled how Phoebe preferred to

keep her emotions in check. If she did need to talk, to decompress after such a personally meaningful surgery, she wouldn't necessarily choose to confide in him. Perhaps he was getting ahead of himself with his imagined emotional connection and his enthusiasm to dream about the future.

Stripping off his mask and apron, Zach left Theatre in search of Emma and Aaron. While he explained to them that the surgery had gone to plan, that, so far, there were no complications, that Poppy would need to spend the next few weeks on NICU, but now that the hole in her heart had been patched closed she would begin to thrive and gain weight, catch up to her twin sister, a part of him worried that he and Phoebe might not be on the same page, emotionally. Where he wanted to discuss the feelings raised by today's surgery and be there to support her the way he hoped they could support each other as parents in the future, the way Aaron and Emma supported each other, Phoebe was still pushing him out of the door. Just as she'd tried to do that first day.

And maybe she was right to keep her emotional guard up. What did he know about making a romantic relationship work? What if they tried to be more than friends and parents and failed, just as his own parents had? He wouldn't want to put their child in the middle of any hostilities. The last thing they needed was to bring all of their respective baggage to their fledgling co-parenting relationship before it had even had a chance to become established.

As he left the hospital, he resolved to moderate his flights of fancy. No matter how well he and Phoebe worked together, no matter how compatible they were physically, how close he imagined them to be, they both needed to tread carefully.

Now that they'd operated on Poppy, his role here at Sydney Central was almost over. Zach was in no position to make promises.

And his role in Phoebe's life? The other night they'd agreed to a temporary fling.

So why was it no longer so straightforward in his mind?

Later that night, Phoebe knocked at Zach's front door, restless energy winding her tight like a spring. It was late, dark. She wrapped her arms around her waist to ward off the chill in the air and tried not to overthink the reason she was standing on Zach's doorstep, spinning out of control.

Facing him in Theatre while they'd worked together on Poppy's long and tense surgery, Phoebe hadn't anticipated how much she would rely on Zach's reassuring presence. His extensive experience, his surgical intuition and encouragement—

all a balm soothing her concerns for baby Poppy and her family.

It was only natural to project those fears, her doubts and questions for the future, onto their own situation given their shared secret—their own baby—and the nature of their work. Except every time she had looked up, Zach had silently communicated his understanding and emotional support in his eyes, as if they were already a parental team as well as a professional team.

That was what had rattled her to the core, because she had soaked up his compassion and comfort like a sponge.

But she couldn't rely on him for her emotional well-being. She couldn't need him at all.

Sucking in the cool night air, she tried to slow down her panicked breathing. It must be her hormones tricking her, exposing her vulnerabilities. Once Zach left Sydney, life would go on as it had been before they'd met. She would revert to operating alone, cooking for one, making her own plans for the baby.

All without Zach.

Before she could register the hollow pang of loneliness that rose up, the door swung open.

Phoebe's stomach swooped at the sight of him. He was so sexy—relaxed and casual in jeans and a shirt, his feet bare.

'Can I come in?' she said as his surprised expression quickly turned to delight.

'Of course.' He beckoned her inside and closed the door. 'Are you okay?'

Scared to witness his eagerness to see her, she nodded, looked away.

Was she okay? Part of her was spiralling, shaken that she already missed him, even though he was standing right there.

'Is Poppy okay?' Zach asked, his beautiful eyes framed by a frown of concern.

'Everything's fine. Poppy is doing really well.' It was only Phoebe disintegrating as she wrestled with the enormity of it all. In those few brief seconds in Theatre when they had watched Poppy's heart, willing it to restart, she'd wanted so badly to reach out and hold Zach's hand, knowing that he understood how she might have been feeling, because they were going to be parents.

Everything would change.

She would no longer just be Phoebe; she'd be Phoebe plus the baby. Even if Zach wasn't always around, he would be a part of their baby's life for ever, as would his family. She would need to build new relationships, welcome the Archers into her new life as a mother, into the baby's life.

Poppy's highly emotive surgery had made Phoebe realise that, as a mother, she would feel her own baby's pain and heartache and disappointment. Only unlike the Wilsons, she would be doing it alone.

No wonder that, overwhelmed, she'd as good as sent Zach away and finished up alone.

As if aware of her inner turmoil, Zach cupped her face and peered into her eyes. 'I'm glad you're here.' He kissed her forehead. 'I wanted to make sure you were feeling okay after the surgery.'

Phoebe's eyes stung at his consideration. He made her feel cared for, almost cherished.

'I don't want to talk about the surgery,' she said, shaking off his concern and embracing the feeling she'd known her whole life. That no one was coming to rescue her, so she had to be strong, self-sufficient. 'I just wanted to see you.'

Because his eyes were full of questions that she didn't want to answer, she leaned closer and placed her hand on his chest. 'Kiss me.'

Distract me from the way you make me feel.

As if he were slowly but surely building himself into the very foundations on which she stood, brick by brick. As if she might crumble when he left.

She must be confusing her fears for the baby's future with her own needs. Understandable after a gruelling day at work.

Zach's lips hovered close, his stare searching hers, as if he wanted to push her to discuss her feelings. Perhaps he needed to express his own, and she was being selfish.

But if they talked, if she voiced how derailed she was by her realisations that her life was about to change in ways she probably couldn't even contemplate, she might need more than another night in his bed. She might need his assurances for the future. A guarantee that in the same way that they'd made their baby together, they would shoulder the responsibilities and soothe their child's hurts and disappointments as a team. To know that he'd be there when it mattered and that she wouldn't have to face the hurdles and uncertainties of parenthood alone.

Determined to block out her thoughts, she gripped his waist and tugged him closer. 'I want you, Zach.'

Playing dirty, she pressed her lips to his neck, nuzzling kisses up to his jaw while her hand snaked under his shirt. She needed the distraction of pleasure. A reminder that this was just a fling, nothing to do with feelings. To guard her heart like never before.

Although their connection was deepening as they spent more time together, although she'd opened up to him about her personal life, their situation remained the same. He was a wonderful man—kind, caring, considerate. But relying on him emotionally in any capacity was simply too risky, went against every lesson on autonomy she had learned in her formative years, abandoned by her father and encouraged by her mother to be self-reliant.

No matter what she might want for her baby, there was no parallel life where she and Zach had met under different circumstances, fallen in love, raised their child together as a family.

There was only here and now. Two people who had sworn off relationships, determined to do the best by the child they had made.

With a groan of defeat, Zach tilted her face, covered her mouth with his, unleashed the passion—life-affirming and distracting—she craved. The minute their lips touched, his coaxing and hers greedy, her ruminations, the doubts and fears and unattainable fantasies that flickered into her mind's eye at her most vulnerable moments, ceased.

She relaxed, leaning her weight into his arms, which held her so tightly she could feel his heartbeat, his rapid breaths, the growing hardness of him against her stomach.

This was what she wanted. This physical temptation had been there since his return to Sydney. Right now, it was the only certainty she had. And when it was over, when Zach left, they could move on, two mature adults who respected one another and would always be connected by the life they'd created.

While their kisses deepened, each one more voracious than the last, Zach's hand cupped her backside, pressing them close below the waist, his other hand cupping her breast.

Her body melted, flooded with heat, her mind blissfully quiet. 'Where's your bedroom?' she said, when she'd dragged her mouth from his and shoved off her coat, letting it fall to the floor.

Bending, Zach scooped her up, one arm at her back and the other under her thighs. 'I'll show you the way.'

He strode down a darkened hallway and nudged open the bedroom door with his shoulder. The sumptuously made bed dominated the room, which was dimly lit with recessed lighting, warm and inviting despite its masculine décor.

Zach placed her on her feet and tunnelled his fingers into her hair, reverently kissing her face, her jaw, her neck as if she were precious, treasured. 'You are so beautiful. So talented. I was proud to work with you today.'

Although she didn't need his validation, Zach's compliments registered, powerful sentiments she tried to block out. Pretty words cost nothing. Phoebe's father must have once whispered quite a few to her mother. But how quickly had those endearments turned bitter, accusatory, justifications for him to leave?

'Don't talk,' she said, yanking at the hem of his T-shirt, tugging it over his head and tossing it aside so she could run her hands over his warm, dark skin, his springy chest hair, the defined muscles that gave him his physical strength so that when he held her, she felt…protected.

But she was strong too. Emotionally. No matter how tough things became when the baby arrived, no matter what the future held, she would survive without Zach.

She would emulate Rosa Mason, raise their child to be independent, happy and confident.

Phoebe's urgency as they stripped off their remaining clothes spurred Zach on. Except once they were naked, side by side on the bed, he slowed things down, his hands thoroughly caressing every inch of her body. His lips exploring all of her sensitive spots. His kisses rendering her weak with need, until she was clawing at him, begging.

'Zach,' she whispered, when he finally covered her body with his, scraped her hair back from her face and stared into her eyes. She was so exposed by the way he looked at her, the way he relentlessly cherished her body, she almost couldn't breathe.

Their hearts thudded together. Phoebe found

herself held captive by what she saw in his stare: desire, respect, understanding, as if he knew her deepest fears and wanted to walk at her side while she fought her own battles.

'I'm here,' he said, and slowly pushed inside her, skin to skin, so there was nowhere left to hide. Zach surrounded her, engulfed her, invaded her, his determined, all-consuming passion rendering her ridiculously close to those hormonal tears that were never far away.

'Don't make promises,' she whispered about the two words she distrusted the most. He was here for now, but he would go, indefinitely. All she could rely on, all she wanted from him, was this moment of pleasure.

But her demand had also exposed her fear, another valuable piece of her most vulnerable self. He frowned, stroking his fingers through her hair. Would he argue the point when he knew as well as her that their time as lovers was finite before they embarked on the more important and enduring relationship of parents?

As he moved inside her, claiming her body with his touch, watching her react to his lovemaking, speaking to her with his eyes, it seemed to Phoebe that they were talking the same language, that he too harboured concerns for the future and understood the potential for messing things up if they weren't both, oh, so careful.

But as the release she'd craved tore a cry from her throat, as she clung to Zach, buried her face against his neck while he crushed her in his arms as if he'd never let her go, Phoebe feared the time for careful had already passed them by.

CHAPTER TEN

STILL DAZED BY the force of their passion, Zach lay beside Phoebe, one hand resting on her stomach over their growing baby. Great surges of desire welled up inside him. Not physical desire, although that was pretty constant in Phoebe's presence, but other intangible desires for things he'd thought he would never want: a family, stability, roots.

Zach relaxed. An emotional day combined with phenomenal sex would release all kinds of happy hormones and endorphins.

'I want to take you shopping,' he said, stroking his fingertips along the bumps of her ribs. 'I thought we could buy some things for the baby.'

The minute he spoke the words, Phoebe stiffened in his arms.

Frustrated that he'd clearly made a mistake by voicing his growing excitement, he added, 'You know me—I like to plan and be prepared.'

And he would soon be heading to Perth for a month before his next overseas posting with Nurture, which had yet to be announced. He didn't want to miss out, didn't want Phoebe to kit out a nursery alone.

But perhaps she felt rushed.

'Unless you think it's too soon.' Propping his head on his hand, he looked down at her where she lay on the pillow next to his, her face flushed and her hair a wild tumble. Breathtaking.

When he'd opened the door earlier to see her standing on his doorstep, all of the warnings he'd told himself to stay emotionally detached had evaporated. He couldn't ignore their growing connection. A big part of him welcomed it. They were having a baby together. Whatever happened in the future, he would always care for and respect Phoebe. If only she'd let him.

'Hmm…' she mumbled non-committally.

Zach bit his tongue, sensing her withdrawal. Perhaps she was simply drained from the emotions of the day. That was why he'd wanted to talk, to share their fears and concerns for the future after Poppy's moving surgery. But the Phoebe who had stepped through his front door had been a woman on a mission to keep tonight about sex.

So why had his simple request to buy a crib together killed the mood?

'I know it's a little early,' he said when Phoebe stayed quiet, 'but I just thought we could shop for things before I leave for Perth.' He smiled, hoping his excitement would be contagious.

'Um… I'm busy this weekend,' she murmured, sounding far from enthusiastic.

Disappointment settled like a boulder in his chest. Was he pushing too hard? Crossing a line? Perhaps she'd prefer to go shopping with her friends or her mother.

'Okay,' he said, stroking her arm. 'I'm not trying to take over. I just want you to have the nursery of your dreams, that's all. Dad tried to foist the Archer family crib on me when I told him about the baby. But as it's been used for four of his children and a handful of grandchildren, it's seen better days.'

'I haven't given much thought to the nursery, to be honest.' Phoebe sat up, clutching the sheet to her chest. 'So I'm um…not sure what I want.' She swung her legs over the edge of the bed and turned her back on him while she searched for her discarded clothes.

Confused, Zach also sat up. He wanted to touch her again, to stroke her back in a soothing gesture, to kiss her and find the fun post-sex vibe they'd shared in Brisbane, but she was clearly in a hurry to get away.

'Phoebe, is everything okay?' After that night at her apartment, after she'd come to him tonight, he hoped her guard was a thing of the past. They'd said they'd be honest.

'Absolutely.' She donned her underwear and stood, scooping up her skirt from the floor without looking his way.

Was he missing something?

'Don't rush off,' he said, wincing at the pleading tone of his voice. 'Have you eaten dinner? I could make you something.'

'I should go.' She tugged her blouse free of the tangled sheets. 'I have an early start tomorrow. There's a press conference being held at the hospital for the Wilsons. Hospital management thought it would be a good idea to field questions on the family's progress, given the unprecedented interest in Poppy's surgery.'

Having slipped on her blouse, she focused on the buttons.

As he watched her don her professional layers as she dressed Zach battled her easy dismissal. The miles of distance she was inserting between them reminded him of that first day in her office. But they'd come so far since then, hadn't they?

'You should come, if you can.' She looked at him then and his stomach tightened at her businesslike tone. 'I'd value your input and it will be good public relations for both the hospital, and your charity work.'

'Sure. I'm happy to attend the press conference,' he said, rising from the bed and slipping on his boxers and T-shirt, while he battled the disconcerting feeling that somewhere along the way he had come to crave more of Phoebe than she was willing to share and the feeling obviously wasn't mutual.

Aware that this loss of control where relationships were concerned was new territory for him, he tried to remind himself that he'd agreed to a fling without feelings. The fact that Phoebe was succeeding at the sex-only plan they'd stipulated better than him made irrational panic squash his lungs.

But he couldn't switch off who he was. He cared about this woman in a way he'd never before experienced. She was carrying his baby. Was he a fool to want to plan and prepare and dream about the near future when they'd become parents, when Phoebe seemed determined to rush out of the door?

Was this how his parents' marriage had soured? Poor communication, mismatched expectations, distance and hurt feelings?

Feeling vulnerable and somehow short-changed, as if his needs were irrelevant, Zach dropped the subject. It was getting late and Phoebe still had to travel back to the city.

He walked to the front door, pulling her into his arms one last time. He kissed her, pressing her back against the wall, cupping her face, sliding his thigh between her legs and swallowing up the mewling sounds she made, the relief that she clearly wanted him physically as much as he wanted her compensation for the niggling thought that she still didn't trust him.

'I'm glad you came over,' he said, when he'd eventually pulled back.

He didn't need Phoebe's permission to shop for their baby, he'd just hoped that he could be an integral part of this pregnancy, in the same way he intended to be in their child's life. But perhaps she still didn't trust that he'd be there for their child. Perhaps she still believed he would let her down.

She stared up at him, and he stroked her hair back from her face, his gaze searching the silvery depths of her passion-glazed eyes. 'I want to ask you to stay the night, but I'm sensing you'd rather not.'

He should be okay that she was leaving. She'd said no promises and he hadn't made any. They'd agreed that keeping boundaries in place was the sensible thing to do for everyone. Except he wasn't feeling sensible. His burgeoning feelings for this woman had left him unsettled, helpless, aware of a looming sense of failure.

Three of his least favourite things.

'I'll see you in the morning,' she said, pressing a final kiss to his cheek before hurrying out into the night.

As he watched her drive away, he told himself that her emotional shielding benefited them both, helped him to focus on what mattered—the baby and the practicalities of their situation—rather than on his feelings for Phoebe. The trouble was, when it came to the latter, he feared he had little control.

And that scared him more than anything else.

CHAPTER ELEVEN

SITTING AT ZACH'S side in the hospital conference room the following morning, Phoebe struggled to concentrate on the question asked by a news reporter from Channel Six, which was fortunately directed at one of her hospital management colleagues.

She was a mess, perfect timing given she faced the assembled press invited to the Wilson family's live press conference. Public concern for the couple and their twins was high in part due to Aaron's celebrity status, but also the house fire that had brought the family into Sydney Central, followed by the dramatic premature birth of the twins and Poppy's congenital heart defect. Flowers, cards and gifts arrived at the hospital by the armload, well-wishes and messages dominating the hospital's social media sites.

Phoebe inclined her head, hopefully giving the appearance that she was fully focused on the discussion taking place, but all she could think about was the man sitting at her side.

Going to his house last night after such an emotionally fraught day had been a big mistake. She'd tried to keep her feelings in check, tried to keep her distance, but if was as if their bond was already so well established that she hadn't been able to hold off the tide of emotions when he'd held her in his arms while they'd made love.

Beside her, he shifted in his seat, softly cleared his throat. She glanced his way, the lure of his stare as impossible to resist as the rest of him. As if they were the only two people in the room, Zach raised his eyebrows the merest fraction in question.

Are you okay?

Relieved to see none of the hurt he'd worn last night when she'd cagily avoided his suggestion to go nursery shopping, Phoebe gave a tiny nod, looking away before she made a fool of herself in front of all Australia by throwing herself into his arms.

After worshipping her body so thoroughly, after cracking open the shell around her heart with his consideration and tenderness, when he'd made the thoughtful invitation the excitement on his face had been the final straw for Phoebe. Too late, she'd realised that she was already in danger with Zach.

She'd failed to stay immune, his attentiveness and empathy combined with the frenzied passion that had followed proving that when it came to her feelings, she was, after all, only human.

But she needed to shove those feelings back inside, to pull herself together, and fast.

'So how long before baby Poppy is discharged?' one of the journalists asked, as if on cue, dragging her attention back into the room.

The hospital's communications manager, who was fielding questions, glanced her way, inviting her to answer.

'We are very happy with Poppy's progress so far,' Phoebe said, her pulse doing a little dance as Zach straightened his tie in her peripheral vision. He looked so sexy in his tailored suit. She wanted to bury her face against his neck and drag in the unique scent of him, which she'd blissfully worn all over her skin to bed last night.

'But she's been through a significant surgery,' she added, her powerless gaze shifting to Zach's as if for his corroboration. 'And while we're hopeful that her post-op recovery will continue without complication, it's still early days.'

Phoebe wouldn't commit to an estimated discharge date for Poppy. The Wilson family had already been through enough turmoil. She wouldn't get their hopes up. It was better to take one day at a time.

'Dr Archer, can you elaborate on the surgery?'

the next question from the audience came. 'Was it technically challenging?'

Phoebe plastered a stoic expression on her face while she listened to Zach's confident voice fill the room through the microphone on the table in front of them, trying to ignore the memory of it throaty with desire and, worse, flat with disappointment at her lukewarm response.

'Any surgery on a neonate of Poppy's size is technically challenging,' he said, looking her way so she had to brush aside the weight of her guilt and nod. 'But fortunately, Poppy had Dr Mason's skill and diligence on her side. That meant the operation passed without a hitch.'

Seeing the pride in his eyes once more, Phoebe wanted to sink into her chair. It was the same expression he'd worn in Theatre yesterday when Poppy's heart restarted and their repair held, the same look he'd worn when he invited her to go shopping for the baby.

While Zach explained the intricacies of the surgery in his clear and concise way, Phoebe choked at the memory of his hand lovingly covering their child.

Of course, a part of her was desperate to nest, to fill her spare bedroom with baby paraphernalia, to plan the décor and build furniture. Now she'd had her first scan, seen the baby in real time, the building excitement was tangible. Were she and Zach a couple, she'd have jumped at the chance to shop together, to paint the nursery together and argue over which screw went where as they assembled the cot. But in reality, they weren't a couple. Zach was leaving Sydney in a matter of days, as he'd reminded her last night, and hadn't once mentioned when, or even if, he might return.

So she'd held back, scared to play happy families when she would soon be alone once more. Forced herself to as good as decline. Dashed out to her car before allowing the inevitable tears to fall. What other choice had she? It would be hard enough to avoid thinking of him every time she looked at their baby, even harder if she laid their baby in a crib they'd chosen and built together. She needed to protect herself, to run away from the feelings she was terrified to analyse in case they told her she was becoming dependent on Zach.

As he finished his explanation of the VSD repair surgery, Phoebe smiled his way. Their eyes locked for a split second, long enough for Phoebe's pulse to go crazy. He was wonderful. This was his baby too. He deserved to feel excited, to ponder names and plan a nursery. She owed Zach more than she was currently offering.

Her attempts at of self-preservation were denying Zach a relationship with their baby, exactly what she didn't want.

He was falling in love with their baby in the same way she was. It was natural, beautiful, a part of who he was. She'd been so focused on him leaving that she'd overlooked how the paternal bond between father and child could be as strong as the maternal one.

Underneath the table, she discreetly placed her hand over their child in the same way he'd done the night before. Their baby would be lucky to have the love and support of both parents. It would grow up knowing three grandparents, aunties and uncles and cousins in a way that Phoebe herself had never known.

No wonder she'd developed an emotional connection to an amazing man she both respected and liked, who she was sleeping with while carrying his baby. That didn't mean she should put scary labels on those emotions, or that they could be trusted, or that she should freak out. She and Zach had a plan to enjoy this fling while it lasted, and then seamlessly transition into parenting together.

All she needed to do was stick to the plan.

'Now that the blood flow through Poppy's heart is moving in a normal direction,' Zach continued, looking to Phoebe before addressing the audience, 'her risk of complications—heart failure, pulmonary hypertension—has greatly reduced. Currently she is still on a ventilator, but she'll have another scan later today to determine her progress.'

Phoebe nodded, adding, 'Poppy is a fighter and she has an amazing team on her side.'

'That's all the questions we have time for,' the communications manager said.

'Before we conclude,' Phoebe spoke, 'on behalf of the Wilson family and the staff at Sydney Central, I'd just like to thank Dr Archer for making time in his busy schedule to return to Sydney. His surgical skills are in constant demand all over the world, so we appreciate that he was able to spare the time to consult on this case.'

Praying that only she'd heard the way her voice broke when she'd said his name, Phoebe averted her gaze from Zach. She didn't want to think about how much time they had left. She didn't want to imagine how bereft she would feel when he walked away. She didn't want to wonder if she'd ever see him again, to watch the door and wait for the phone to ring the way she had as a confused little girl missing her father.

As the press conference ended, she stood and quickly ducked out of the room. The past twenty-four hours with Zach had tugged her in all directions. She needed to unpack her feelings in private so she could face him without the urge to beg him to stay.

* * *

Zach chased after Phoebe, his longer strides catching up to her clipped pace along the corridor while his heart thundered. Why had her vote of thanks just now, on top of her leaving his place last night, sounded like a goodbye speech? And why, when they'd both always known that his time here in Sydney was temporary, when he had responsibilities in Perth, patients relying on him, was he chafing at the idea of ever being anywhere else?

'Phoebe, wait!' he said, touching her arm to snag her attention. She smiled, but not quickly enough for Zach to miss the hint of anguish in her eyes.

He knew her now. She could no longer hide from him the way she'd been doing since that first day. But despite everything they'd been through with the baby and working together, despite him feeling closer to her than ever last night, she was still pushing him away.

'Do you have a second?' he asked. 'Can we talk?'

Why was she already as good as shoving him on a plane? Why was she reluctant to talk about baby names and shop for the nursery? Why had she left his bed last night, while he'd lain awake for hours, covered in her scent and wishing she were back in his arms?

'Of course.' She put her hands into the pockets of her lab coat and glanced along the corridor.

Zach released an internal sigh at her closed-off body language. Perhaps the question he should be asking was why he kept presenting himself for rejection. Just because he never gave up, was he taking his self-belief too far? He'd never done this before. What if pushing her to open up destroyed what they had? Perhaps any relationship between them, because of his commitment issues and Phoebe's lack of trust, was doomed to failure.

What then? What would that mean for their child? He knew first hand from watching his parents' marriage implode how being caught in the middle felt.

'Why don't we um…talk in my office?' she said, looking nervous, as if she expected him to pounce on her at work. Part of him wanted to do that very much, to loosen her pulled-back hair, to kiss her until her eyes glazed over with passion the way they had last night, to hear her whisper his name with the same desperation.

But a bigger part of him wanted answers to the questions he just couldn't silence.

Zach followed her to her office, his lips pressed together, to stop himself from saying something that would push her further away, the way he had last night.

Inside, she closed the door behind them and

turned to face him. 'Zach, I want to apologise for last night, for my lack of enthusiasm for shopping. I was tired. Poppy's surgery really took it out of me, but I want you to know that I'd love for us to go shopping for the baby together.'

Zach nodded, momentarily stunned by her turnaround. 'No need to apologise. I'm happy that you like the idea.' Deciding that there was no time like the present, he pushed on. 'I wish you hadn't rushed off last night. Poppy's surgery was emotional for me too. A first in fact. I couldn't stop projecting hypothetical concerns for our baby, and I wanted to ask if you'd felt the same way. Understandable given the nature of our work.'

She nodded, her eyes misting, so he stepped close and slid his hands around her waist. She gripped his biceps, looking up at him with so much uncertainty his heart felt bruised.

'I did feel the same,' she whispered. 'Which is why my apology is very much needed, Zach.' She rested her hand on her stomach. 'This is your baby too. You have just as much right to choose nursery furniture and names, to have concerns for the unknown and to be excited for the future.'

She looked down, snagging her bottom lip with her teeth as if ashamed. 'I might have lost sight of that for a second, and I'm sorry.'

Because he couldn't stand the vulnerability

in her eyes, because it felt natural and he was done questioning why, he tilted up her chin and pressed a soft kiss of forgiveness to her lips. 'This is a complex situation for both of us. It's okay that we're making it up as we go along.'

She nodded, rested her head on his chest over his galloping heart. He held her close, sucked in the scent of her shampoo, closed his eyes, wishing this moment where she was leaning on him for emotional comfort could last for ever.

'I know you're scared to rely on me,' he said, gripping her tighter because she stilled in his arms. 'I know that your trust is a hard-won thing, and I know you said no promises. But—' he pulled back to stare into her eyes, needing to say it anyway '—I promise to always do my best to be there for you and the baby, whenever either of you need me.'

'Thank you,' she whispered.

He wanted to say more, to confess that he was convinced the only viable solution to this co-parenting thing was for him to reside permanently in Sydney. But if the idea of one shared trip to the baby store had freaked her out, she wasn't ready to hear his thoughts on relocating. Because every time he imagined himself living here, full-time, he also imagined him and Phoebe continuing to date.

Swallowing, he willed his heart to slow. She

wasn't interested in a relationship. He didn't know how to make one work. There was no guarantee they could make it as a couple. If they tried, they might ruin what they were trying to build for the baby: stability, an amicable co-parenting situation. Romantic feelings only ruined relationships, led to disappointment and bitterness and affected everyone else in the firing line. Their child deserved better than that, and Zach would do everything in his power to ensure that he or she was happy.

'I've been thinking—' she looked up at him with wide eyes '—about your parents. Do you think they'd want to meet me? As they live in Sydney too, they'll want to spend time with our baby.' She shrugged. 'I might even need their help.'

Feeling as if he'd won a skirmish in an epic battle, Zach grinned. 'Of course they will want to meet you. You're the mother of their future grandchild.'

'Okay, good. I just wasn't sure because, you know, we're not a couple, but if you think it's a good idea…'

'I had hoped that once you get to know them, you might feel comfortable enough to ask them for support, if I'm not around.' A strange hollowness expanded inside him at the thought of Phoebe, the baby and his parents spending time together while he was elsewhere, as if he were being torn in two, limb from limb.

She nodded. 'I look forward to meeting them.'

'I'll ask them for some dates they're free that might work for you.' Zach smiled, a kick of primal emotion under his ribs. He admired her independence, respected her self-sufficiency, but these small gestures gave him hope. He knew how hard it was for her to lower her guard and rely on others.

She was so strong but was genuinely trying to embrace all of the changes to her life that the baby would bring. Because he couldn't stop himself, he cupped her face, kissed her lips, her cheeks, the tip of her nose and her closed eyelids.

She stood on tiptoes and curled her arms around his neck, pressing her mouth to his, parting her lips and touching her tongue to his, turning a sweet kiss passionate. As was the way of their chemistry, their embrace escalated, their hands roaming each other's bodies, each of them panting, as if they couldn't find enough contact for satisfaction.

Phoebe's sexy little whimper brought Zach to his senses. He dragged in air and slowed things down, pressed chaste kisses to her lips.

'Sorry about that,' she said, resting her forehead on his chest as she gripped his arms. 'These hormones are making me insatiable for you.'

Zach chuckled. 'Well, I'm here for that, whenever you need me.'

She laughed, joyful and unguarded. Zach's spirit soared. He wanted to put that look on her face every day, until she believed that he wouldn't let her or their baby down.

'What did you want to see me about?' she asked, bringing him back to one of the reasons he'd chased after her.

'Oh, yes. I wanted to invite you to a fundraiser next weekend. It's the Nurture Neonatal Trust annual ball. I was wondering if you'd like to go.'

'Aren't you leaving for Perth that weekend?'

'I leave on the Monday.' Zach shook his head, wishing he could cancel his commitments. This fragile new understanding between them felt important, a breakthrough. He should be here for the scans and the introductions to his family. But just because he was slowly earning Phoebe's trust, just because for a moment last night, when she'd lain in his arms, their heartbeats crashing together, he'd had the fleeting urge to hold onto her for ever, didn't mean he should risk spoiling this good thing they had going.

Better to excel at one thing than risk failing at two.

At his reminder, her eyes clouded over, increasing Zach's guilt. 'In that case I'd love to go, although I might have to wear a loose-fitting gown. My skirts are becoming tight in the waist.'

Zach slid his hands to her hips, tugging her close, fantasising that they could sneak home and spend the day in bed until everything slotted into place. 'So does this Saturday work for you? For the crib shopping?'

She winced. 'I'm sorry. I can't this weekend. I have plans. It's my friend Ivy's hen party.'

Zach braced himself against the wave of disappointment. 'Okay.' The days were disappearing fast. He wanted to spend as much time as he could with Phoebe before he left. But of course she had commitments too.

'Want to see some patients?' she said, tucking some escaped hair behind her ear.

'Let's do it,' he said, this chat leaving him hopeful that they would work everything out. Work was always a good distraction.

But as they headed to the NICU, their first stop on Phoebe's ward round to check on Poppy, Zach couldn't help but feel that, up to now, he'd used his work to find solace for the gaping hole in his personal life. Why else would a part of him be dreading leaving Sydney?

In the past, that had never bothered him all that much. So why had it changed? Reluctantly, he acknowledged the answer: Phoebe.

CHAPTER TWELVE

THAT WEEKEND PHOEBE closed her eyes and tried to relax back into the sumptuous leather chair while the masseuse massaged the instep of her foot with divine-smelling lavender and geranium oil. This day at Serenity Spa with the girls was just what she needed to settle the tumult of emotions she'd experienced since Zach had come back into her life. Sleeping with him again while grappling with some major realisations that, despite thinking she had everything all figured out, her life would never be the same, had unleashed all kinds of unsettling thoughts and amplified her already fragile emotional balance.

Hopefully this fun and relaxing weekend, after a week where she and Zach had worked together by day and made love every evening, neither of them acknowledging the loud countdown of his remaining time in Sydney, would set her back on a more emotionally stable path.

As if sensing Phoebe needed a distraction from her thoughts, bride-to-be Ivy, who was undergoing the same foot treatment in the next chair, said, 'I could get seriously used to this. Perhaps I should get married more than once, or marry someone who owns a beauty spa.'

'Except you're madly in love with Lucas,' Ali said as Phoebe and Harper chuckled.

'Oh, yes.' Ivy giggled. 'There is that small point to consider.'

Phoebe sighed with contentment at the love and camaraderie around her. 'You are all so revoltingly loved up.'

As she beamed down the row of pedicure chairs occupied by her friends, her heart fluttered. They all deserved the love they'd recently found, Harper seizing her second chance with dishy Yarran, Ivy finding Lucas after having her heart broken by her cheating ex, and divorced Ali blissfully happy with her adrenaline junkie, Jake.

Thinking about her friends' love lives only amplified her sad lack of one, because her temporary sex life didn't count. Except sometimes when Zach held her, or kissed her tenderly, it seemed as if he was about to say something… momentous. What would it be like to be loved by a man like Zach, a man who gave his all to his passions, a man who, if she could believe his promise, would never let down their child the way Phoebe had been abandoned and repeatedly let down by her own father, who should always have been there for her, even if his marriage to her mother had failed?

In those moments, she dared to imagine that he wanted more than the fling they'd agreed on, unleashing fantasies of her and Zach and their baby together as a family.

But just because they were going to be parents, just because he loved his child, wanted to be in his child's life, didn't mean he wanted to be romantically involved with Phoebe. Neither of them had any experience of making commitment work.

Her fantasy was flawed for heaps of reasons, not least of all that Phoebe knew better than to pin her hopes for happiness on another person.

'You looked sad, just then, Phoebs,' Ivy said, reaching across the space between their chairs to take Phoebe's hand. 'Don't worry, Lucas has four single male cousins who are coming to the wedding. We'll soon have you fixed up, loved up, shacked up—'

'Knocked up,' Harper added, and she and Ivy burst out laughing.

Phoebe smiled weakly, her stomach taking another swoop when a member of the spa staff appeared carrying a tray of champagne flutes. 'Champagne, ladies?'

The others murmured their delight, each taking a glass and leaning over to clink them together in celebration of Ivy's hen do. Phoebe fought the panic beating at her chest. She should have anticipated there'd be alcohol, that she'd need to make yet another excuse. But given she'd had to abandon her jeans this morning for a loose-fitting skirt, she reasoned there was no more hiding it from her friends. Any day now a pair of eagle eyes would notice her tiny baby bump, and she was tired of lying to them by omission. The jig, as they said, was most definitely up.

Time to come clean to Ivy and Harper.

'Could I please have something non-alcoholic?' she said to the staff member, avoiding the curious glances of her friends.

'We have sparkling elderflower cordial. Does that sound good?'

'Lovely, thanks.' Phoebe waited until the woman had left the room before turning to face her friends.

Three sets of eyes watched her, waiting. Ivy and Harper's brimmed full of curiosity, and Ali's were soft with sympathy and a hint of excitement.

Phoebe smiled at all three of them, dragging in a fortifying breath. 'I absolutely don't want to make a big deal of this. It's Ivy's day. She's the reason we're all here. But I'm not going to be able to hide it for much longer, and you've probably guessed anyway. I'm pregnant.'

She exhaled a breath shaky with nerves, reasoning that she would need to get used to saying it aloud, given that she'd have to apply for maternity leave soon, not to mention all of the hospital staff who'd be offering their congratulations. A tremor of apprehension rattled thorough her. Not only would she be telling her mother face to face later this week when she visited Rosa, she'd also agreed to meet Zach's parents.

Speechless, Ivy beamed at Phoebe, her green eyes dreamy.

Harper nudged Ivy's arm. 'I told you so.' Then added to Phoebe, 'Congratulations. I am so excited for you. I'm going to be an auntie.' She placed her champagne on the arm of her massage chair and clapped her hands with glee.

Phoebe laughed, covering her mouth and blinking away the silly burn of tears as she stared at her friends, women she couldn't imagine being without.

'I'm happy for you, too,' said Ivy, her hand flat on her chest as if she was struggling with her emotions.

'Thank you.' Phoebe sagged with relief. Now that her friends knew, she only had to worry about telling her mother. 'Now that you all know, there's no need to talk about it further. We can get back to Ivy's hen party.' She settled back in her chair, hoping the subject was closed.

'Whoa, hold on,' Harper said, turning to face a sheepish-looking Ali. 'You knew?'

Ali, shrugged, momentarily cornered. 'I was sworn to silence—doctor-patient confidentiality. But thank goodness I no longer need to keep a secret from you guys.' She collapsed back into her chair dramatically. 'That was torture.'

Ali and Harper laughed together, showing the depth of their healed bond after their past falling out.

Phoebe smiled, her heart swelling now that all four of them were close once more, the way they had been at med school. Really, life was good. With these wonderful friends on her team, once the baby arrived, she felt confident that everything, including her new platonic relationship with Zach, would fall into place.

It had to.

'Wait, who's the father?' Ivy asked, her eyes shining with so much excitement, Phoebe squirmed with discomfort. No doubt her friend wanted the same happily ever after for Phoebe that she and the others had found for themselves.

Only a relationship—love, marriage—wasn't for everyone. Life sometimes gave you lemons. Phoebe would just be the odd one out of the group.

Strangely deflated by the idea, she imagined facing Zach every time he came back to Sydney to visit the baby. Would she be over their fling? Or would she miss his arms? His kisses? The way he cared?

'It's that Zach guy, isn't it?' Harper said, a gleam of satisfaction lighting her hazel eyes. 'I knew there was something going on when I saw the way the two of you kept gawking at each other at the press conference. He's totally into you.'

He was into her for now. But he'd soon be gone, indefinitely, with no mention of returning. 'There's nothing going on,' Phoebe said, blinking rapidly, refusing to succumb to tears today. 'But yes, Zach Archer is the father. We had a one-night stand at the conference in Brisbane.'

Even saying the words gave Phoebe butterflies in the pit of her stomach. Rather than working the physical cravings from her system, their lovemaking only intensified with every night they spent together.

But those nights with Zach were numbered.

'So you're not an item?' Ivy asked, a small frown of confusion on her face. 'Is he with someone else?'

'Of course not,' Phoebe said, pierced by white-hot shafts of jealousy at the idea of Zach moving on. But of course he would at some stage. He was a virile single man. He would meet someone else.

How would she face him and a new date, perhaps arriving to pick up the baby for an outing, and not want to stamp her ownership all over him in indelible ink?

Except he wasn't hers…

Slapping on the upbeat mask she wore when cornered, she turned to her friends. 'You know me, I'm not looking for a relationship, and neither is Zach.'

But maybe one day he'd change his mind, meet a woman he couldn't live without, look at her the way he looked at Phoebe but actually say the words that Phoebe sometimes heard in her fantasies.

'So what about the baby? Have you talked about how you're going to raise him or her?' Ali asked, using her compassionate doctor's voice, which left Phoebe wanting to pull the hood of her robe over her head and hide.

'We're going to co-parent. But Zach travels a lot, as you know, so we'll have to see how that works out.' Could her friends hear that tremble in her voice? Could they see the secret fear she had barely acknowledged herself, that, by going it alone, she was making a huge mistake?

I promise to always do my best to be there for you and the baby, whenever either of you need me.'

The problem was, she didn't know how to rely on anyone, having spent her entire life being self-sufficient and sceptical of any vow made by a man. She'd had no choice but to rely on herself.

'So you're not sleeping together?' Harper asked with a degree of intuition that made Phoebe's skin crawl.

She blushed, a slave to her hormones once more. 'Um…well…yes, we are, but only until he leaves the week after next. It's purely practical.'

To distract her friends from their line of questioning, and herself from daydreaming of a future where she and Zach were an item, she offered them a mischievous smile. 'He's pretty good at that, and I'm a bit hormonal.' She shrugged, laughing when Ali fanned her face, impressed.

Ivy clapped her hands excitedly, and Harper just stared, gobsmacked.

Glad that she'd managed to shock her friends into silence, Phoebe accepted her glass of elderflower cordial from the staff member and took a long, bolstering sip. For now, she'd navigated a big hurdle by coming clean to Ivy and Harper, but if she knew anything about her friends, it was that her reprieve from their searching questions wouldn't last for ever.

The Serenity Spa had a wonderful outdoor swimming-pool complex, complete with sauna and hot tub. The entire area was set among shade-offering trees, a veritable jungle of shrubs and flowers adding to the tranquil oasis vibe. While Ivy and Harper relaxed in the hot tub, Phoebe and Ali sat in the shade of an enormous umbrella on comfy poolside loungers. Phoebe had taken a swim, but the sauna and hot tub were a no-no. She didn't want to come over all faint again and embarrass herself or ruin Ivy's day, and her *news* had already dominated enough of the hen do.

Wondering if she might find something in the spa boutique to wear to Zach's Nurture fundraising ball, Phoebe rested her hand over the slight swell of her stomach, giving way to the building excitement of impending motherhood, while she wondered if this was the last time she'd be able to wear a two-piece. Her mother had developed extensive stretch marks during her pregnancy, so Phoebe would probably do the same. Not that it mattered. No one would see them but Phoebe.

'I think he's good for you, Phoebs,' Ali said from behind her closed eyes. Like Phoebe, she wore one of the spa's fluffy white robes over her bikini as they dried off from their swim.

'Who?' Phoebe asked, playing dumb.

'Zach.' Ali opened her eyes, levelling a serious look Phoebe's way. 'I've never seen you so… radiant.'

Phoebe scoffed, uncomfortable with the idea that Zach was responsible for her glow, if indeed she had one. 'It's the hormones,' she bluffed.

'They're a blessing and curse, I assure you. One minute I'm euphoric, the next I'm crying because there's a cute kitten on my social media feed.'

But Ali was right. Zach had changed her life. Not only when they'd conceived the baby, but he'd also helped her to come to terms with the idea that her world was about to be turned upside down.

'It's not just that,' Ali pushed, sitting up to look Phoebe in the eye. 'You seem happy, light-hearted. It suits you.'

Her friend was fishing in her subtle way, giving Phoebe a chance to examine the vagaries of life. Ali had never wanted children, and Phoebe would never have imagined that she'd become a mother at forty. But thanks to Zach, with every passing day she became more and more excited to meet her baby. Of course, she'd have to make it through the birth first.

'I probably won't be so composed when I'm surviving on no sleep, have cracked nipples and baby blues.' Staring at her new pedicure, the coral-pink nail varnish on her toes, Phoebe wondered for the millionth time where Zach would be on the baby's due date. She deliberately hadn't questioned him on his schedule, assuming that he would be overseas, working for Nurture. Would he make a special trip back to Sydney for the birth of his baby? Or would the absence make him change his mind, go back on his word and decide that the demands of fatherhood were just too much trouble after all?

No, Zach was going to be a great father.

'You know that you don't have to do it all alone, right?' Ali said, her dark eyes searching.

That was the trouble with friends you'd had since childhood: they knew you too well, had witnessed you at your best and worst, were privy to your darkest fears and sometimes your greatest hopes.

But Phoebe had barely allowed herself to imagine what those might be for herself, the sneaking suspicion that they involved Zach making her shy away from examining the fantasies too closely.

'I know.' Phoebe faked a broad smile, trying to keep the conversation light. 'By the look on Ivy's face earlier, I'm certain I'll have plenty of offers of help. Plus I want you all to be godmothers, so no shirking your baby-minding responsibilities.'

'We'll all be here for you, Phoebs.' Ali swung her legs over the edge of her lounger and faced Phoebe. 'But you know that's not what I meant. See, this is what you do.'

Uh-oh—now she was serious.

As she stared straight ahead to avoid Ali's no doubt sympathetic expression, her focus blurred. Ali intended to have her say, and a part of Phoebe welcomed her friend's viewpoint. Except she was used to being the captain of her own ship, those habits hard to change. And an even bigger part of her was terrified that her friends would think she was making a big mistake by giving up on Zach.

Being a parent was hard. Being a solo parent, twice the challenge. But a baby alone wasn't enough of a reason for two people to be together. She would never want him to resent her in the future because he felt…trapped.

'What do you mean?' she asked, her stomach hollow with trepidation.

'I mean, my darling, that sometimes you have this tendency to push other people away, even us, your friends.'

Phoebe gaped, appalled. Did she? If so, she didn't do it consciously…

'You know that I'm not used to asking for help,' Phoebe said, icy fear trickling through her veins at the thought that maybe Zach would think the same thing. Now, backed into a corner, forced to think about the vulnerabilities that stemmed from her childhood, her needs beyond her job, the fleeting dreams of a fantasy future that she usually dismissed, she felt that sickening feeling return, like the gnaw of hunger.

Except it was fear.

'I know that you're a strong and capable woman,' Ali said, 'who, quite rightly, doesn't need a man to feel whole. We all love that about you. But Zach seems like a really decent guy.' Her voice turned softly persuasive. 'Jake remembers him from med school, said he's ambitious and driven, but straight as a die.'

'I know,' Phoebe whispered, her brain awash with memories of the kind, considerate and passionate man who'd literally turned her world upside down, firstly back in Brisbane when one night of incendiary chemistry had created a life, a little piece of her and a sprinkling of him, and then again with his constant emotional support, his quiet acts of chivalry, his inexhaustible sense of humour. When he devoted his time and energy to something, be it her pleasure or making an omelette, he did so with the dogged persistence she had once thought was arrogance, but now recognised as one of his greatest strengths.

Zach committed.

'I like him too,' she confessed, just saying the words bringing her out in goosebumps of terror. Her throat burned with unshed tears. But just because he'd been there for her this past couple of weeks, just because he'd vowed to be there for their child, didn't mean that she could trust him with her heart, put it on the line and suggest they have a proper relationship. She'd never trusted anyone that way, always ensuring her own soft landing.

'But relationships take effort,' she said, glanc-

ing away from the empathy in Ali's stare. 'Even
when there's a child involved, a strong reason to
make it work, relationships fail. You know that,
and I know it because of my parents. Zach too
has divorced parents, and they have four children together!'

It wasn't just her feelings to consider; it was
about the baby, too. She needed to be stronger
than ever for their child. She and Zach couldn't
afford to mess this up.

Taking her silence as permission to continue,
Ali said, 'I know, and I'm in no way suggesting that you haven't already thought all of this
through, but if you get on well enough to work
together, to sleep together, to plan to raise a baby
together, don't you think there's enough there on
which to build a relationship? People get together
on the grounds of much less.'

'Perhaps.' Phoebe nodded, watched Ivy and
Harper climb from the hot tub and head for the
outdoor showers.

She turned to her friend. 'But neither of us has
risked a committed relationship before, and in all
the time we've spent together, we haven't talked
about the possibility. I think that's because we've
both figured out that if we try to have more and
fail, we'll ruin things for the baby. Zach's parents put him in the middle when they split. He

wouldn't want to inflict the same on his child, and I respect him for that.'

'But it's not just about the baby, is it?' Ali urged. 'The two of you are also individuals who deserve happiness in your own right.' Scooting closer, Ali touched Phoebe's arm. 'What do you want? In here?' She pressed her balled fist to her chest, impassioned.

Phoebe shook her head, bewildered now that she'd been forced to think of the one thing that had thrown her into confusion this past week: the desires of her heart.

'I don't know,' she whispered, scared to admit that she'd spent years ignoring the emotional demands of that organ. 'I keep going around in circles. I can see the logic for both sides of the argument. Alone is what I know. But Zach and I have so much in common and we'll be raising the baby together anyway...' She sighed, deflated. Her world was more topsy-turvy than ever.

Ali tilted her head sympathetically. 'You know that I love you and I'll support you, always, whatever you do. But I'd hate to see you throw away a chance to be a family with Zach because you're scared, hung up on being...practical.'

Phoebe smiled, laughed through the tears stinging her eyes. 'I guess you make a good point.'

'Think about how you feel when you're with

him,' Ali continued. 'And then figure out what you want, for yourself, not just for the baby's sake.'

Phoebe nodded, wiping her eyes. A flutter of excitement formed under her ribs, telling her that Ali's reasoning spoke to some long ago shutdown part of Phoebe. Her friend was right. She could open herself to the idea of a relationship with Zach and examine what she truly wanted. They were good together and she had nothing to lose by just considering the possibility of a relationship.

But would Zach even be interested? Would he be willing to change his lifestyle for her? Even if he wanted to try and have a relationship with Phoebe, he would struggle to find the time, given his current work schedule...

There was long distance and then there was simply impractical. She didn't want to become something holding him back, someone to blame when the pressures of family life, something Zach had never craved, took him away from the work he loved. Resentment and bitterness would kill any relationship stone dead. Wasn't it better to keep her guard up, keep things non-committal and focus on their plan to raise the baby?

Hearing her mother's deeply ingrained words— *'never rely on a man'*—she swallowed the lump of fear in her throat and looked away.

Across the pool area, Ivy was headed their way, a big smile on her face, leaving Harper under the outdoor showers.

'Can we finish this discussion another time?' Phoebe said. 'I want today to be all about Ivy.'

'Of course,' Ali said, mollified.

Slapping a smile on her face, Phoebe waved at Ivy, glad for the distraction and reprieve from thinking about Zach.

'I've had the most brilliant idea,' Ivy said, sliding into her robe and wrapping her head in a towel turban. 'I'm going to message Lucas and ask him to invite Zach to the wedding. If he's going to be the father to my future godchild, I think we all need to get to know him a bit better.'

She smiled triumphantly and Phoebe's heart sank.

'It's your wedding.' Phoebe smiled weakly, her insides a mess of anticipation and dread. 'You're the bride.'

There was no way out, unless Zach declined the invitation. But would he fly back from Perth just to be Phoebe's plus one?

Without looking at Ali again, Phoebe lay back, closed her eyes, pretending to relax while inside she ticked like a time bomb. Having Zach as a guest at the wedding all but labelled them a couple, and part of her understood her friend's desire for a bit of harmless matchmaking.

The invite would prompt a conversation about him returning to Sydney. Maintaining the status quo, denying the need to think about her feelings and what she truly wanted, was the coward's way out. She'd never thought of herself that way, but the alternative, deciding that she wanted more with Zach and presenting the idea to him, seemed a sure-fire way not only to open herself up to his rejection, but also to ruin everything they were planning.

As Harper joined them and they headed to the changing rooms to dress for lunch, all Phoebe could think about was how neither solution suited her, that she needed a plan C and couldn't for the life of her come up with one, and that was her biggest problem of all.

CHAPTER THIRTEEN

THE NURTURE NEONATAL TRUST was an international charity whose aim was to standardise best practices in global neonatal care. Zach had undertaken pro bono work for them for the past six years in far-flung places where access to cutting-edge neonatal surgery was limited by poverty or politics.

Zach had always found the work highly rewarding.

But as he took Phoebe's hand and led her to the dance floor in the ballroom of the Sydney Sails Hotel, he couldn't imagine anything would ever beat the feeling of having Phoebe on his arm.

She looked stunning in a full-length black beaded gown that hugged her figure, showing off her slight baby bump. And although he didn't normally bring a date to these functions, preferring to network, this evening, knowing that she was carrying their child, seemed way bigger than a date.

As he pulled her into his arms, their secret

warmed his chest. He had the urge to announce to the entire room that this wonderful, caring, smart woman was not only with *him*, but would also be the mother of his child.

Phoebe laughed up at him as he spun her around. She fitted into his arms as if she were made for him, as if they were empty without her, as if, together, they were somehow…two halves of a complete whole.

'You look absolutely beautiful tonight,' he said, resting his cheek against hers, the crush of feelings in his chest all but choking him.

'You said that at my place and in the car.' She chuckled, her blue eyes alight with excitement and mischief.

Zach gripped her tighter. 'It's worth repeating.'

He locked eyes with her, the urge to kiss her so strong, he almost did. But public displays of affection might prompt questions Phoebe wasn't ready to answer. She lived and worked in Sydney. He didn't want her subjected to gossip or to make things awkward for her after he left for Perth Monday.

Her heart thumped against his. 'Well, I'm definitely showing now.' She glanced down at her stomach. 'Especially in this dress.'

Zach smiled weakly. They hadn't discussed breaking the news about the baby wider than close friends and immediate family. It was

Phoebe's call who she wanted to know in her workplace. But the part of him more and more convinced that he wanted to ask her to give their relationship a chance was desperate to tell the world.

'How did your mum take the news?' she asked, looking up at him, her blue eyes emphasised by smoky eye make-up, so he feared that she might be able to see deep inside his soul.

And what would she see there? His desire, his excitement, but also his fear. Fear that she would reject him. He was a major risk for her, perhaps if tonight went well, he'd take her home, make love to her and pop the question.

He'd never done this before—built a romantic relationship. But just like when he'd operated solo for the first time, if he applied his intuition and drive, he'd surely get what he wanted.

He wanted Phoebe.

'Both of my parents are overjoyed for us,' he said in answer to her question as he recalled their delight and congratulations. 'And as I predicted, they can't wait to meet you.'

She smiled hesitantly at first. 'Really?'

Zach nodded. 'Of course. They even re-watched the press conference when I told them that you were sitting next to me. I also told them you were keen to meet them too, but they understood that you have a busy schedule.'

Of course, his mother had also bombarded him with the inevitable unanswerable questions he'd expected. Like, *'Why aren't you together?' 'Have you considered proposing?' 'Don't you want to be a family?'*

At the time, Zach had easily dismissed them. But after, in the quiet solitude of his apartment, missing Phoebe and wondering how the hen party was going, he'd forced himself to come up with answers.

Not to the impractical marriage question, at which he'd rolled his eyes, but as he'd mulled over the reasons they weren't an item, he'd grown more and more convinced that they should be one.

Now he just had to choose his moment and persuade Phoebe.

As if relieved, Phoebe exhaled with a small shudder. 'So it's really happening, then? No going back now.' She laughed it off, but there was a nervous edge to her voice.

'It's really happening.' He held her a little closer, his hand flat between her shoulder blades, because whenever he was with her, close just didn't feel close enough.

Looking up at him, she sobered, chewing her lip. 'I finally told my friends Harper and Ivy last weekend at the hen party.'

Zach kept his surprised reaction from his expression, knowing that for Phoebe, as for him, spreading the word might have invited other people's opinions on their co-parenting plan and how that might be…triggering for someone with her trust issues. 'How did they take it?'

'Good.' She sounded overly reassuring. He guessed that she'd probably faced similar questions about the baby's father. 'They asked about you, of course,' she confirmed. 'They're all very supportive. I'm lucky to have them in my life.'

'They're lucky to have you, too,' he said, staring deep into her eyes, spying her vulnerability there.

She paused, nibbled at her lip and stiffened slightly in his arms. 'Ivy said she planned to invite you to her wedding next month.'

'She has,' he said, sensing Phoebe's discomfort at the idea.

'You'll still be in Perth,' she stated, her voice carefully emotionless. 'Don't feel as if you have to come back for it. It's a major hassle for you. I think my friends just wanted to know you a bit better as we're going to be in each other's lives as parents.'

Parents, not lovers or a couple…

Seeing a return of the wariness he thought they'd put behind them, Zach hesitated. As maid of honour, she was an important part of her friend's wedding party. If his presence at the event was going to make her uncomfortable, to raise questions about them, perhaps he should stay away.

'I already accepted, with the proviso that my commitments might change,' he said, trying to keep his hurt and disappointment that she didn't seem to want him there from his voice. He'd been about to ask her what she thought of the idea, but she obviously hadn't invited him to be her plus one.

'I said I would let them know as soon as possible if I couldn't make it back,' he added, trying to salvage the wrong turn his dream evening had taken with Phoebe's clear apathy.

Composed, as if she had no preference either way, Phoebe nodded and glanced away. 'So tell me about your work for Nurture,' she said, changing the subject.

Zach bit back a groan of frustration as yet again she put a slice of emotional distance between them. Was he alone in his feelings for her, or perhaps he just needed to give her some more time?

Zach explained the international work the charity undertook and then added, 'The work is so rewarding it doesn't feel like work, you know. I see places that I wouldn't normally travel, see real people living very different lives in very different places from the life we take for granted.'

Staring up at him, she smiled as if seeing him for the first time. 'I can see that it means a lot to you.'

'I've been a part of it for many years.' He shrugged. 'They have fifty-six branches all over the world. If possible, they either fly the patient to the nearest tertiary centre or fly in the relevant specialists. The cases are varied, often rare, the presentations unusual.'

She smiled up at him, her expression impressed, and Zach realised he might have overdone his enthusiasm. 'That's amazing, Zach.'

It had been an amazing experience for a man without personal commitments. But of course all of that was about to change. Zach was looking forward to the next chapter of his life as a father, probably his greatest challenge, because, just as he'd promised Phoebe when he'd first found out about the baby, he wanted to give his all to fatherhood.

As the dance came to an end, Zach led Phoebe towards their table. At the edge of the dance floor they were stopped by a colleague of his, Debbie Ellis, a Sydney-based anaesthetist who had also volunteered for Nurture for many years.

'Zach, it's so good to see you on our home turf,' she said, standing on tiptoes to press her cheek to his in greeting.

'Debbie, this is Phoebe Mason from Sydney

Central.' He smiled, placed his hand in the small of Phoebe's back in that possessive way that was now second nature.

Phoebe tensed.

Zach immediately dropped his hand. Clearly she wasn't interested in anyone thinking they were together. His stomach twisted with the fear that, despite the fact that they had spent most of the past two weeks constantly together, maybe he and Phoebe were on entirely different pages, emotionally.

'Debbie is an anaesthetist at Harbourside Hospital,' he explained, desperate now for the evening to end so they could have a meaningful conversation about their future.

The two women shook hands and the three of them chatted for a while, discussing the dire traffic situation in the city and the plans for a brand-new hospital in the eastern suburbs.

'So, have you heard? Nurture is sending you and me to South America for four months,' Debbie said, raising her glass to Zach.

'No, I hadn't heard.' Zach kept his composure while his heart banged. 'I thought Nurture were announcing their upcoming projects after dinner tonight.'

He glanced at Phoebe, who quickly adopted a serene smile that made his teeth grind. But he'd seen her flicker of dismay, the doubt and disappointment.

Did she honestly believe he'd go to South America for four months when their baby was due? Did she still think so little of him that her expectations of him as a father were still on the floor? And if she still believed him capable of running out on her and their child that way, she must also believe that he had no feelings for her at all, perhaps because she had none for him…

Trying to reassure Phoebe with his eyes, he changed the subject. Nothing was yet confirmed. Zach would wait for the official announcement by Nurture. But even if Debbie was privy to inside information, Zach had the option to decline the work offered him by the charity. And on this occasion, decline it he would.

With a tight smile, Phoebe excused herself and headed for the ladies' room. Zach watched her retreat, his stomach full of lead. He'd always planned to return to Sydney for the birth of his baby. He'd even been imagining some sort of happy family fantasy, where he announced he was staying in Sydney and Phoebe welcomed his news with open arms and declared that she wanted them to have a relationship. But from the look on her face as she'd turned away just now, his fantasy couldn't be any further from reality.

* * *

Phoebe entered the hotel room Zach had booked for the night, her feet hesitant, as if she were made of glass and one wrong step would see her shattering into tiny shards on the plush carpet.

She'd never felt so conflicted. Trying not to think about how their lovely evening had soured, she kicked off her heels and placed her bag on the table.

Zach's vague answer about attending Ivy's wedding had been the first warning siren. But the news that he'd be spending the last trimester of her pregnancy in South America had knocked the breath from her lungs. It had taken every scrap of her energy to choke down her heartache and jealousy and appear unaffected, to smile and laugh and clap her way through the rest of the evening, which had begun with such promise when she'd danced in his arms and allowed herself to dream that maybe they stood a chance.

But fairy-tale endings weren't for everyone. Hadn't she always known that? Except somewhere along the way, she'd forgotten.

As if aware of her fragility, Zach gently reached for her hand and tugged her into his arms in silence. Could he tell that she was one kiss away from begging him not to leave on Monday? But she would never ask him to choose between embarking on a relationship with her and the work he so clearly loved.

Raising her lips to his, she kissed him, blocking out the searching look in his eyes and the clamour of feelings she'd only there, on that ballroom dance floor, finally acknowledged.

She wanted all of Zach. She wanted them to take what had begun as a physical fling and build on it through trust and honest communication, through everything they had in common, through love for their child. Her friends had been right. They had as good a shot as anyone else of making it.

But that had been before she realised exactly what was at stake if she confessed her dreams for the two of them and asked Zach to return to Sydney. He would have to choose—her or his charity work.

She just couldn't do it, in case he chose his career, in case he returned out of a sense of duty and later regretted it.

'Phoebe,' he groaned, pulling back from the heated passion of their kisses. 'We should talk.'

While she slid his tux jacket from his shoulders, she trailed her lips along his jaw and down his neck, knowing the distraction would make him shudder.

'After,' she said. 'I want you, Zach. Seeing your colleague kiss you made me jealous.' She admitted the truth, tugging his shirt from his waistband and sliding her palms against his skin, followed by the light scrape of her fingernails, because these past weeks as his lover had taught her that it drove him crazy.

'She's just a colleague,' he said, his eyes stormy with desire for her. 'I'm focused on you and the baby, only interested in *you*.' He slid open the zip of her gown and she stepped out of the garment. 'And before you ask, no, we've never slept together.'

'I had no intention of asking such a personal and intrusive thing. Who you've slept with in the past is none of my business, Zach.' Nor was his future.

Because a personal conversation might break her, she undid the top buttons of his shirt and tugged it over his head, pressed kisses to his bare chest. If this was goodbye, she wanted to be with him one last time, to imprint every second of the night on her memory so the next time she saw him, whenever that might be, she might stand a chance of being over him.

'What if I want it to be your business?' he said, dropping his head back, exposing his neck to her kisses. 'What if I want more of you than sex? What if I want to fall asleep with you in my arms, to wake up with you there too, to make you breakfast and hold your hand?'

As if carried away by the fantasy, he groaned, banded his arm around her waist and hauled her flush against his chest. He pressed kisses along her collarbones and over the tops of her breasts, which were still encased in her strapless bra.

Phoebe closed her eyes and surrendered to his touch, blocking out his words, shoving aside the mental images he'd created. They formed a pretty picture, but, in reality, it wouldn't work out. There were too many obstacles to navigate. Their priority had to be the baby. Phoebe didn't want her child—*their* child—to grow up the way she had, not knowing its father.

Between the baby's happiness and her own, the choice was an easy one.

They moved to the bed, their passion burning out of control, as always. Phoebe pressed her lips all over Zach's body, tasting his skin, absorbing his sighs and groans, making him restless, driving him to desperation until he growled, scooped his arm around her waist and slid his body over hers.

'I won't go,' he whispered, breaking the rules, staring down at her while their hearts thundered together, chest to chest.

She had no idea if he meant to Perth or to South America, but it didn't matter. He must have sensed her turmoil. Perhaps he too realised that this was their goodbye.

'Shh,' Phoebe said, shaking her head and silencing him with a kiss. The part of her that Ali had forced her to examine, the part of her that at the start of the night had been certain she wanted a relationship with Zach, was desperate for his promise to be true, for it to be what he wanted.

But tonight's words wouldn't be enough. At some point in the future, those heartfelt intentions, whispered in the throes of their passion, might turn to bitter resentment, especially when his time and his loyalties were torn between the career he loved and the sacrifices he'd made.

She couldn't ask it of him, not now, not ever.

'Make love to me, Zach.' Wrapping her legs around his hips, she clung to his shoulders. He trailed kisses down her neck, took one sensitive nipple into his mouth and then the other, driving her wild until she forgot all about holding something back from him in order to protect her heart.

She gave him everything, allowed her emotions to brim in her stare as he pushed inside her, his lips seeking hers once more, his hand roaming her thigh, her hip, her waist and her breast before cupping her face and drawing her closer to his kiss.

'Phoebe, I want us to talk,' he said between snatched breaths as their tempo built. 'I have things I want to say.'

Even now, near the height of desire, Zach showed the determination she admired.

Balanced on the precipice of her orgasm as they stared into each other's eyes and he moved inside her, she nodded her agreement. The time for the conversation she'd been putting off was almost there. If only she could avoid it for ever... stay in his arms for ever.

As they climaxed together, Phoebe buried her face against his neck, blinking away the sting of tears in her eyes. As she clung to him, she feared that she was falling for Zach, in spite of everything. But she couldn't fall. Instead, she had not only to let him go, but also to push him away, one last time.

Her final act of self-preservation.

CHAPTER FOURTEEN

ZACH STROKED HIS fingers through the soft silk of Phoebe's hair, enjoying the feel of her sprawled naked over his chest. His heartbeat hadn't yet returned to normal. He doubted it ever would. How could it when he was strung too high, his feelings for the woman in his arms, the woman he'd decided earlier tonight in the ballroom downstairs that he couldn't live without, crushing his lungs like blocks of concrete?

How had he managed to hold them inside for so long? And how could he release those feelings slowly enough so he didn't scare Phoebe away? Because ever since the conversation with his Nurture colleague, he'd sensed her slipping from his grasp.

'I want us to date,' he said, laying it on the line without preamble. Why had he forgotten that as soon as he saw something he wanted, he went after it? He was Zach Archer. He aimed high and always achieved his goals.

And no goal had ever meant more than Phoebe.

'Zach…' she whispered, sounding resigned, as if she'd been expecting some kind of revelation from him and had a logical let-down speech already prepared. 'It's not going to work.'

'Why not?' He tensed, refusing to accept her pushing him away until he'd told her how he felt.

'For the same reasons that it was never going to work,' she said, sitting up and clutching the sheet to her nakedness. 'I live here, and you don't. Neither of us has any experience at making a committed relationship work, and, most importantly, we agreed when we started this fling that we'd put the baby first.'

Her arguments were sound, leaving little room for disagreement. Except his desires wouldn't be silenced by reason, by a pact made when his feelings for this woman were only one fraction of what they were now. 'We can still put the baby first and make time for each other. Couples do it all the time.'

Phoebe sighed and then faced him, gorgeously sexy, achingly beautiful and absolutely determined. 'And you don't think that trying to start a relationship when we live in different cities, different countries, when we have demanding jobs, when a newborn baby has to be our number one priority, is going to make it impossible?'

Zach stared, giving her arguments proper consideration. But all he came up with was how she'd written them off before they'd even had a chance to start. The same way she'd written him off as a father back in the beginning. But maybe that was the problem. Her fear of rejection was making her scared, that was all.

Zach gripped her hands, desperate for her to understand his point of view. 'I haven't agreed to go to South America. I can decline. I can move back here after my time in Perth and—'

Before he'd even finished speaking, she began shaking her head. 'No. I think you *should* go to South America. Your charity work is important to you, Zach. I saw that this evening. You know that I'm not going to stop you from seeing your child when you return, or ever, but the baby alone is no reason for us to be together.'

'Wait a second,' he spluttered. Where had that come from? Did she think that he only wanted to be with her so he had access to his child? After everything they'd been through, her opinion of him was still in the gutter, as if she didn't know him at all.

'I'll be fine taking care of the baby by myself until you return to Australia,' she ploughed on, 'and then we can discuss the arrangements, visitations, custody, all of that.'

'I want to discuss it now, Phoebe.' Pressure built in his head. This wasn't going how he'd planned. 'This isn't just about the baby; I want you too.'

He cupped her face and urged her stare back to his, so he could search for her true feelings beneath the fear. 'You're just scared. I am too. I know neither of us has done this before, but we can make it work. We can make anything work.'

Unless he was wrong. Unless he'd been the only one to risk his heart and Phoebe had kept hers safe. She'd been pushing him away from day one. But how many more knock-backs could he take? How many hints did he need before he admitted defeat? Maybe in the same way his parents' relationship had ended, he and Phoebe just weren't meant to be...

'And what if we can't, Zach?' Her eyes turned stormy, desolate. He wanted to hold her until she believed in him the way he believed in himself, the way he wanted to be there for her, always.

'What if our relationship goes the same way as my parents', or yours, or my friend Ali's?' she continued, pragmatically, slamming up barrier after barrier. 'What then? I don't want our baby to be fatherless. I don't want them to wonder if it's you every time the phone rings or when someone knocks on the door. To only half enjoy their birthdays because they have one eye watching and waiting for someone who is never going to turn up, because, just like your parents, we can't be in the same room any more.'

Zach winced, her throwing back that snippet of information he'd shared with her in a vulnerable moment a stinging slap in the face. 'I told you that I'm not that man,' he gritted out, his voice falling ominously calm. 'I'll always be there for my child. Always.' Although he didn't want his child to be exposed to the atmosphere of bitterness and resentment Phoebe suggested was inevitable.

In his head it was very clear. These were two separate issues. But she didn't want to hear his feelings. For her this was clearly still a physical relationship.

'I know you will,' she said, her expression sincere and passionate, as if he was missing some vital part of her argument. 'And I'm so grateful that our baby will have you in its life. That's exactly what I want, Zach. I want you to be the amazing father I know you're going to be. I want our baby to know he or she can rely on you, always, that you won't let them down. Ever.'

'But you're not willing to risk the same for yourself? To trust me when I say I'll figure things out and always be there for you too?'

Deflated, she sagged. 'Is it worth risking what we have now—a respectful relationship, two people committed to raising this child, giving it the best of everything we can give? Isn't it better to focus on making that work? Better for all of us. You, me and the baby.'

Zach opened his mouth to speak and closed it again. How could he argue with that? She made sense. If he could rewrite his own history, would he take two parents who could communicate without resentment, without putting their children in the middle, over two who'd loved each other but then watched that love burn out and turn to ash?

It was obvious that Phoebe had no feelings for him beyond the respect she talked about, otherwise she'd be willing to trust him, to give them a shot at a proper relationship.

Perhaps she was right, perhaps it was better her way…

'You know I'm right,' she said, her voice flat. 'Believe me, I wish it were as simple as giving us a try, making it up as we went along. But we're not a couple of teenagers. At least this way…' she reached for his hand, placed it over the swell of her stomach '…no one gets hurt, including our baby.'

Zach clenched his jaw, defeat a sour taste in his mouth that he'd never liked. Clearly for Phoebe it was black and white. They could parent together, but she just wasn't willing to take a risk on him when it came to her own heart.

He could fail at one thing or fail at both. The choice was his.

CHAPTER FIFTEEN

A SUMPTUOUS AFTERNOON tea at Betty's café was a ritual Phoebe and her mum looked forward to whenever Phoebe made the trip home, as she had two weeks after Zach's departure. But as their waitress deposited a three-tier cake stand full of yummy goodies on the table and left, Phoebe doubted that she'd be able to eat a single thing for the nerves robbing her appetite.

'So I wanted to ask you a favour,' Phoebe said, diving right in before Rosa Mason noticed that Phoebe wasn't attacking the delicious delicacies with her usual gusto.

'Darling, you can ask me anything, you know that,' Rosa said, pouring tea for them both into fine bone china floral teacups.

Rosa was about to cut her scone in half, when Phoebe dropped her bombshell, too nervous and distracted to sugar-coat it.

'Can you recommend a good midwife in Sydney?' She smiled weakly, fearing Rosa's reaction

to the news she was about to become a grandmother.

Her mum's knife clattered against the plate.
'Are you pregnant?'

Phoebe nodded, nerves fizzing in her veins.
'Yes. I'm around nineteen weeks.'

While Phoebe sucked in air and waited for
her mother's response, Rosa covered her mouth
with her hand. 'Oh, my goodness.' She rose from
her seat opposite Phoebe and gave her daughter
a hug. 'Oh, darling, that's wonderful news. I'm
going to be a grandmother.' Rosa's eyes filled
with a sheen of moisture.

Phoebe sagged, relieved at Rosa's elation. 'I
wanted to tell you in person, not over the phone,
but I've been so busy at work,' she said, explain-
ing the delay.

'I can't believe it. I'm in shock. I didn't even
know you were seeing someone.'

Phoebe's empty stomach took another dive.
'I'm not, Mum.'

Her personal life was a mess.

Rosa blinked in confusion. 'Oh… Well, how
very modern of you, darling. Did you use a
donor?'

Phoebe sighed, searching for the strength to
explain the complexities of her situation with
Zach and deciding the truth was best. 'No, it was
nothing like that. I had a one-night stand. He's

a neonatal surgeon. We met at that conference I attended in Brisbane.'

As if she'd set aside thinking about Zach after the Nurture ball, as if he'd merely been waiting in the wings of her mind to make a grand re-appearance, Phoebe once more saw his hurt expression as clearly as if he were sitting across the table.

Rosa's eyes widened with excitement. 'He's not that lovely doctor who operated with you on that tiny Wilson baby is he? The one from the press conference?'

Phoebe had had no idea her mother had even seen the media coverage of her involvement with the Wilson family. 'Um…yes. Yes, that's him—Zachary Archer.'

They had parted maturely with a goodbye kiss and he'd left for Perth. And ever since, Phoebe couldn't shake the feeling that she'd done something terrible.

'But you're not seeing each other?' Rosa frowned, her expression just like those of Ivy and Harper when she'd explained it to them that day at the spa.

'Well…we have been seeing each other, but he's left Sydney now, so we won't be seeing each other again, aside from when we parent together. Separately, obviously.'

Spoken aloud, with her feelings all over the

place, the situation that had seemed so complicated became ridiculously simple.

Why weren't she and Zach a couple? He wanted it, she wanted it. It made so much sense. Of course she'd made a huge mistake in rejecting Zach's suggestion that they date seriously. Why else was there a big gaping hole in her chest, as if she had misplaced something irreplaceable?

'I guessed there was something between the two of you when I saw the way he doted on your every word on the news.' Rosa nodded sagely, glancing at Phoebe in her Mum way.

Phoebe tried not to squirm. 'Mum, he did not dote on me.' It didn't matter if it made sense. She'd deliberately, consciously pushed Zach away without stopping to truly listen to what he had to say, and now it was too late. He was gone, already in Perth and unlikely to return any time soon. Why would he when Phoebe had given him nothing to return for?

'Oh, well, you know your own life best, darling. I'm just saying what I saw when you looked at each other. I know what love looks like. It was obvious to anyone with eyes that he's smitten with you.'

Love? Had she fallen in love with Zach? A buzzing noise sounded in Phoebe's head.

Oh, no… She loved Zach. That was why she

was so completely terrified to give him an inch. She loved him and he could really hurt her.

'I take it he knows he's going to be a father?' Rosa said, with that hint of accusation Phoebe had heard many times before whenever Rosa mentioned Phoebe's father.

'Of course he does.'

'But what, then?' Rosa said, her voice growing shriller. 'Has he done a runner?'

'No. It's not like that, Mum,' she hissed, leaning closer, the urge to defend Zach strong and instantaneous. 'He's going to be a great father. He's so excited. He wants to go shopping for a crib and baby clothes. He wants to choose names and to introduce me to his parents. And I—'

I ruined it.

'And you what?' Rosa waited, her scone untouched, her tea going cold.

'He wanted us to have a relationship and I pushed him away.'

'Ah,' Rosa said, her voice tinged with sympathy. 'I understand now.'

'What do you understand?' Phoebe swallowed, desperate for her mum to make it all better the way she had when Phoebe was a little girl.

Rosa's gaze softened as she tilted her head. 'That you're scared to trust this man with your heart.'

Phoebe nodded. *Terrified.*

'Can you blame me,' she whispered, 'when the only example I've ever known was my father, the man who broke yours?'

Rosa winced and reached for Phoebe's hand in understanding. 'Your feelings are your feelings, darling. And while your father wasn't a great role model, we were very young when we got together. We probably shouldn't have rushed into marriage. You are a strong, mature woman who knows her own mind. If this Zach fellow, who by the way sounds lovely, has earned your love, I have no doubt that he deserves it.'

'He is lovely,' Phoebe admitted, glancing down at the tea she was too grief-stricken to touch. Not only had she fallen deeply in love with him, if her mother was to be believed Zach might be as crazy about her, and she'd thrown him away.

What had she done? How could she win him back?

'Do you regret falling in love with a man who let you down so badly?' she asked, fighting the urge to catch the first flight to Perth.

Rosa considered the question Phoebe had never before asked. 'No, because if we hadn't met, hadn't rushed into our relationship, we wouldn't have made you. You were the best thing your father and I ever did together. My only regret was that he wasn't mature enough to be the father you needed.'

'I have everything I've ever needed in you, Mum.'

Rosa blinked away tears. 'You are going to be a wonderful mother. You and Zach sound well suited, but I'm certain that you will figure out a way to be wonderful parents, together or apart. And I'll be there to support you, whatever you choose to do.'

Phoebe nodded, torn in all directions. She couldn't rush to Perth to tell Zach she'd messed up, changed her mind, loved him. She had work—Poppy Wilson was off the ventilator and doing so well she was likely to be discharged this week—Ivy's wedding, her maid-of-honour duties.

'And I say this to all my first-time mums,' said Rosa with an encouraging smile. 'To be the best mother you can be, you have to tend to your own happiness, too.'

Phoebe hid the panic catching her breath. She had finally worked out what she needed to be happy: Zach. Except thanks to her fears holding her back, he was so far out of her reach, he might as well be working on the moon.

After a long day of surgeries at Perth Memorial Hospital, Zach shuffled into his barren hotel room without turning on the lights. Despite the lack of reminders in the anonymous room, he sensed Phoebe everywhere. He might as well be back in his Sydney apartment, where the rooms echoed with Phoebe's laughter, her scent lingering on his bed sheets, and the box of tea he'd bought because she could no longer tolerate coffee sat in the cupboard, mocking him for his foolish dreams.

It didn't matter that physically she was four thousand kilometres away. It was as if he'd carved out a Phoebe-shaped space in his chest and carried her with him when he'd left.

Except she didn't want him in return.

She'd chosen safety over him, kept her emotions locked away. Dismissed his suggestion that they try to make their relationship work as if it had already failed.

And scared of the failure she seemed to think was inevitable, he'd caved.

Why had he given up without a fight? When he wanted something, when he believed in a course of action, he chased it to the end, made it happen, succeeded.

And he'd never wanted anything more than he wanted Phoebe. Maybe that was the answer. The stakes were higher, the risk of failure more devastating because he was in love with her.

Stunned with disbelief, he stepped into the en suite bathroom and started the shower on autopilot, tossing his scrubs into the laundry bin and rubbing at the pain behind his sternum.

Was this love? The endless obsession with her in his thoughts, the constant desire to be close to her, this ache in the centre of his chest that had more than once these past two weeks made him worry he was having some sort of cardiac event?

Sick at the possibility that he'd fallen in love with a woman who'd consistently knocked him back, Zach gripped the edge of the sink and dropped his head. Maybe an icy cold shower would freeze the heartache and he would be able to rationalise that Phoebe had been right. It was better to focus on their relationship as parents, one they just had to make work.

Just then his phone rang. His heart lurched, concern that it was Phoebe and something was wrong his first, terrifying thought.

Snatching it up from the bed where he'd dropped it, Zach saw it was his father. He took some deep breaths and picked up.

'Hi, Dad. Is everything okay?' Zach willed his pulse to settle, now convinced that this feeling of utter futility, of wanting to crawl out of his skin, must be love. He loved Phoebe and he'd walked away because he was scared to fail.

'Hi, son,' Henry Archer said. 'All good here. I'm just coming back to you with some dates that might work for meeting Phoebe. Sorry that it's taken me a few days. Work has been very busy.'

Zach's empty stomach turned to lead. He'd forgotten that he was supposed to be arranging a time for his parents and Phoebe to meet. Only now that things between them were more distant than ever—a few polite texts, the odd email— would she still want to meet his parents?

Trying to ignore the concern that by telling her he wanted a relationship before he'd left Sydney, he'd ruined what they'd already had, doomed their chance at an amicable co-parenting arrangement, Zach winced. 'That's great, Dad. Thanks,' he said, making a note of the weekends his father was free over the next couple of months.

Phoebe wanted the best for their child. Neither of them would allow anything to get in the way of that, but Zach also wanted her for himself, for his own happiness, for ever.

Zach scrunched his eyes closed as he listened to his dad ramble on about something inconsequential, his stomach turning for what felt like the millionth time since Phoebe and him had said goodbye.

Why hadn't he realised that he was in love with her sooner and told her that? Had some part of him, the competitive part that always needed to be the best, held back from complete honesty, fearing that deep down he lacked the skills to make a committed relationship work? Had he done exactly what he knew would trigger her own fears by letting her down, giving up when things became too hard?

'So when will you be back in Sydney?' Henry asked, dragging Zach back into the conversation.

'I'm um…not sure, probably another two weeks.' Zach glanced at his suitcase in the corner, indulging in his daily fantasy of packing up early and flying back to Phoebe. But his surgical schedule at Perth Memorial was booked out for at least the next two weeks with cases that had waited months for his visit, patients and their families relying on him to honour his commitments.

'That doesn't sound like you, son,' his father said. 'I've never known you to be uncertain of anything.'

Oh, Zach was certain of some things. He'd declined the trip to South America with Nurture, opting instead to undertake some Sydney-based work. Whatever happened with Phoebe, whether she wanted him or not, Zach would stay close by so he could be there for both her and the baby.

'Yeah, well, you know exactly how life sometimes trips you up.' Zach laughed bitterly.

What he really needed was to see Phoebe again, to tell her in person that he wasn't giving up on them, that he'd always be there for her, that the most important ingredient to any relationship's success was love. He loved her. He should have told her that.

Curling his hand into a fist with frustration, he waited out the loaded seconds of silence on the other end of the phone. 'Is this to do with Phoebe?' Henry Archer said with surprising insight. 'Are you having relationship problems?'

Zach gritted his teeth, wishing things were that simple. 'We're not together, Dad. I told you that.'

'Well, your mother and I talked, and—'

'Wait! You and Mum talk?' Zach gaped, mind blown. 'Since when?'

Zach sank onto the bed, the assumptions he'd made about his parents' marriage and divorce shaken as if the whole hotel were being rocked by seismic activity.

'Yes, we do, when it concerns the welfare of one of our children,' his father said. 'You'll understand that now that you're having a baby of your own.'

'What I don't understand,' Zach said, trying to get to grips with the fact that he'd built his whole relationship belief system around the example set by his parents, only for it to morph before his eyes, 'is you and Mum talking, when you can no longer stand each other.'

'Nothing is ever that simple, Zach. I respect

your mother. She's a wonderful woman. She gave me four amazing children.'

'But…' Zach deflated. Stunned speechless. But what if all this time he'd focused on the wrong thing, the fear that a relationship might fail? What if, when it came to relationships, to love, he should trust his intuition the way he did in the operating theatre? Now that same intuition was screaming that he'd made the biggest mistake of his life in not fighting harder for Phoebe.

He wasn't a quitter. He always got the job done. If she had no feelings for him, he deserved to know, but he also owed it to himself to tell her how she'd changed his life.

'So what did you and Mum discuss about me?' he asked, his jaw aching from grinding his teeth.

'Well, we watched that press conference on the news, and your mother rang to say she thought you'd finally fallen in love and to ask if you'd confided in me.'

Zach opened his mouth to deny it, but closed it again. Had it been that obvious to others? But just because he loved her, didn't mean that she returned his feelings.

'I'm sorry if the breakdown of my relationship with your mother hurt you, Zach. I know things weren't easy for you during the divorce and, for that, I apologise. Your mum and I had many wonderful years of marriage before growing apart.

And one thing we've always agreed upon is how proud we are of our family. All we've ever wanted is for all four of you to be happy. I guess we both feel that it's been hard watching you fill your time with work, but neglect your heart.'

Stunned, Zach said nothing. His father was right. He had neglected his personal life.

'I have absolute faith in you to make the best of any situation, son. You always do,' his dad said. 'If you say that you and Phoebe are better off co-parenting, then I know you'll make it work. Just always be true to yourself, that's all I ask.'

'Thanks, Dad,' Zach said, the hollowness inside him expanding as he acknowledged his truth. He wanted more than the practical co-parenting relationship he'd allowed Phoebe to convince him was as high as they could reach. He wanted it all. He wanted his family to be together: him, Phoebe and their baby. He wanted to take care of Phoebe, to cook for her and dance with her and make love to her until she realised that she would always be able to rely on his love.

Now he just had to wait until he could confront Phoebe face to face, to see into her eyes when he told her that he loved her, and hope that it wasn't too late.

CHAPTER SIXTEEN

Two weeks later

IVY'S BRIDAL GOWN was a close-fitting lace sheath that hugged her figure to the knee and then swished in an elegant fishtail as Lucas, tall and handsome in his tux, swirled his new bride around the dance floor. As the next song began, an upbeat cover version of an old sixties classic that had everyone joining the bride and groom for a boogie, Phoebe discreetly left her seat.

Fighting off the waterworks once more, she ducked out of the exquisitely decorated ballroom where the wedding reception was being hosted and headed to the bathroom. Locking herself in a cubicle, she collapsed back against the door in relief and sniffed into her last tissue.

Why were weddings so emotional, every *ahh* moment amplified by her hormones?

Ivy and Lucas's ceremony had been beautiful, their personal vows leaving not a single dry eye in the congregation. But now that they were officially man and wife, now that the cake had been cut and the speeches were over, Phoebe took a moment to indulge in a tear or two for her own shattered dreams.

She wasn't going to have her own happy ever after.

Pressing her hand to her chest, where the burn of grief was strongest, she relived the less celebratory parts of the day, how she'd watched the door, willing Zach to appear. It was a test she'd set herself, a bargain. If he came to the wedding, it meant that he might be open to giving her a second chance. She'd planned to take him aside, tell him that she'd changed her mind, that she wanted them to make their relationship work. Who knew, she might have even plucked up the courage to tell him that she loved him...

Only she'd woken up to that realisation too late. He was in Perth thinking that she had no feelings for him, because she hadn't been able to put them into words during their few shared texts. Now she'd never know what his response might have been, because he hadn't shown up, and she couldn't blame him for his absence.

She'd obviously pushed him away one time too many.

Swallowing convulsively, she looked up at the ceiling, blinking rapidly. She would be okay. Just as Rosa had for her, Phoebe would ensure that her and Zach's baby was happy and healthy, no matter what. And just because he wouldn't be a part of Phoebe's life in the way she wanted, she knew Zach would move mountains to always be there for their child.

Resting her hand over her baby bump in a silent promise to their little one that he or she was going to be the luckiest baby alive, Phoebe dried her eyes and tossed the tissue into the toilet.

For the first time that morning Phoebe had felt the baby move, a slight fluttering feeling, like bubbles popping. Her first instinct had been to call Zach, to share the wonderful, miraculous news and excitement with him, knowing that he'd be as awed as she had been. Her hand had even reached for her phone, and then reality had come crashing down on her once more. She'd thrown away the right to call him, to rely on him emotionally, to share her fears and dreams with him, when she'd thrown his gentle proposal that they date in his face.

By indulging her doubts that a relationship between them might not work out, she'd rejected Zach, and, in the process, ruined her chance for her own happy ending. Now she had to go it alone, just as she'd told Zach she could in the very beginning.

Because she couldn't hide in the toilets all night, licking her wounds, she left the cubicle and washed her hands, grateful that her waterproof mascara meant she'd avoided panda eyes with all the welling up. Facing her reflection, she thought of Rosa's ringing endorsement.

Phoebe *did* know her own mind. She wanted more for herself than her fear had allowed her to reach for. She wanted it all with Zach: a wonderful father for their child *and* a loving and committed relationship for herself. She deserved it all, just like her friends. Her deep-rooted belief that she was somehow unlovable because the man who'd donated half her genetic material had abandoned her had shaped her thinking for far too long. It was time to move out of her own way and use her independence to go after her own dreams.

But what if it was too late?

She couldn't leave Ivy and Lucas's wedding reception yet; this was Ivy's special day and she was a maid of honour.

Maybe she could book a flight to Perth for first thing in the morning…

Deciding to head outside for a breath of fresh air, for five minutes away from the party atmosphere to pull herself fully back together, she bypassed the ballroom and slipped outside through the nearest exist into the cool night.

The ballroom opened to wraparound terrace, which was strung with a million twinkling fairy lights, like stars. Phoebe selected the far corner, away from the few guests who'd wandered outside for a break from dancing. With her plan to track down Zach and confess her feelings taking shape, Phoebe breathed a little easier. Soon she would be able to face her friends, to enjoy the rest of the evening, to dance, and see Ivy, Harper and Ali happy without being crushed by the devastation that, through her own foolishness, Zach wasn't by her side.

'Phoebe, are you okay?'

Phoebe turned to see Ali approach, wearing a frown of concern on her beautifully made-up face.

Phoebe nodded, determined to stave off further tears. 'I'm fine, just standing here trying to figure out why I've allowed fear to dictate my life for so long. Why you could see it that weekend of Ivy's hen party and I couldn't.'

Ali wrapped an arm around Phoebe's shoulders. Their heads rested together, side by side, while they shared a moment of understanding. 'We're all slaves to our fears. Are you talking about Zach?'

Phoebe nodded. 'Yes. Before he left for Perth, he said he wanted us to have a relationship and I self-sabotaged, just because I don't know how to do that. Because I've always been on my own, cherished my independence like some sort of lonely badge of honour. But Zach was right. We had something special and I should have been brave, given us a chance.'

Instead, she'd dismissed a wonderful man, a man who, time and time again, had proved he could be relied upon. A man who not only shared her career, but also shared her dreams. A man who'd been willing to make himself vulnerable and explore what had started as a fling but had the potential to be so much more.

'It's not too late,' Ali said, her voice soothing, giving Phoebe's seed of hope wings.

'I don't know, Ali,' she whispered, terrified that hope wouldn't be enough. 'Perhaps it *is* too late. I thought he might come to the wedding, that I could tell him how I feel, but he didn't show up. I ruined it. What if he can't forgive me?'

There was a pause, a few beats of loaded silence that made Phoebe's skin crawl.

'I think you'll still have that chance to tell him how you feel,' Ali said, pulling away and glancing over Phoebe's shoulder.

Phoebe frowned, the hairs on the back of her neck prickling to attention. She shook her head. 'He's in Perth,' she said, confused by the expression on her friend's face.

'Is he?' Ali said, backing away, her nod of encouragement full of inside information.

Phoebe turned back to the ballroom, to where Ali had been looking, her heart in her throat.

Zach skidded to a halt at the entrance to the ballroom, pausing to catch his breath having just run from the underground parking garage as fast as he could. While his heart pounded, his lungs on fire, his gaze frantically sought Phoebe, darting left and right over the darkened room, which was in full-blown party mood.

There were at least twenty round tables, lavishly set for ten people, each bearing a large floral centrepiece, which obscured his view. Determining that Phoebe wasn't among those few people seated, he focused his search on the dance floor, where flashing lights obscured the faces of the people dancing.

Frustration coiled in Zach like dynamite about to blow. He wanted to raise the lights, stop the music and commandeer the microphone, demanding the location of Phoebe Mason, as if it were a matter of life or death.

In some ways it was. He loved her. His heart was dying without her. He'd tried to get through these past weeks in Perth without her and he was adamant that that kind of existence was definitely not living.

Making his way closer to the dance floor around the edge of the tables, he scanned the moving crowd, trying to identify faces.

Panic gripped his throat.

What if she'd already gone home? What if she'd fallen ill? What if she was here but refused to hear him out?

Why had he allowed that missed opportunity

to pass him by? He should have told her how he felt that day of the Nurture fundraiser when she'd lain in his arms. Instead of trusting the powerful emotions, trusting his gut instinct, he had shied away from confessing how deeply he'd fallen in love.

But now he wasn't giving up without a fight. He'd go to her apartment. He would find her one way or another. Beg for a second chance.

He cast his gaze around frantically, his heart lurching, as if it had always known Phoebe's location.

He spied her through the windows. She was outside, being comforted by her friend Ali, each of them wearing matching deep red gowns.

Ice rushed through his veins. He ran outside, stopping in his tracks as Phoebe turned around.

Before he had a chance to register how stunning she looked, her neck exposed by her hairdo, her strapless gown revealing her pale shoulders and the small but noticeable swell of a baby bump, he swept his doctor's eye over her from head to toe.

'Are you okay?' he asked, breathless from the run and the panic that maybe something was seriously wrong.

'I'm fine,' Phoebe said, her reassurance restarting his heart. 'You're here. I thought you were in Perth.'

Ali seemed to have slinked away, leaving them alone.

'I was. I rushed back. For you.' He didn't want to talk about the endless journey following his final surgery. He wanted to hold her, to kiss her, to get down on his knees and beg her to give him a chance to prove that his love could be relied upon.

'You look beautiful,' he said, awed by how stunning she was, inside and out. He stepped closer, because he just couldn't stay away.

'Thank you,' she said, blinking up at him as if she couldn't believe he was real, giving him hope.

'Phoebe.' He gently gripped her upper arms, his nervous system abuzz at the contact. 'I know that everything you said last time we saw each other made sense, that focusing on being parents is the safest course of action, that we should put the baby first, but the thing is, I don't care about safety. I don't care about being scared of the future. I care about you. I love you. I want to be with you. For ever.'

Swallowing hard, he searched for all of the flowery words he'd recited on the endless-seeming four-hour flight from Perth.

'For the first time in my life,' he blurted, urging her to hear him, 'I don't have everything all figured out, which in itself is pretty terrifying. But I promise you that I know how I feel.' He balled one fist and rested it over his heart. 'I love you. I want you. I want the three of us to be a family, a proper family. I can figure everything else out—a new job, where we'll live, which lightweight stroller you prefer from the shortlist I've made. None of that matters. I just can't be without you. Please say you'll give me a chance to keep my promise to love you for ever and always be there if you need me?'

Because her eyes filled with a sheen of tears and because she was too far away, he cupped her face, tilting her head so he could draw her close and still keep eye contact. 'Not that you do need me, or that you have to need me, but please say you'll let me be there for you, just in case.'

To his delight, she laughed, tears spilling free onto his thumbs. 'Of course I need you. I love you too. I want you too. And I want us to be a family, because we already are, Zach.'

'You love me?' he whispered, his heart trying to beat right out of his chest.

She nodded.

He swooped, pressing his lips to hers, kissing up the salty taste of her tears, pouring his all into showing her what she meant to him. 'I love you too.'

'I'm sorry I pushed you away,' she said. 'I'm sorry that I was scared to rely on you. But I know your heart, Zach. I know that you'll always do your utmost. I know that I can depend on you and I'm committed to us, too. You're right—we'll figure everything out, because being without you just doesn't work for me.'

Because her words touched his soul, because, with her love, he was the best, most complete version of himself, because he was dangerously close to begging her to marry him, right here on this balcony at someone else's wedding, he peppered her face with kisses—her jaw, her eyes, her nose and then her lips again.

Phoebe wrapped her arms around his neck, their embrace turning heated as she pressed her gorgeous body against his and parted her lips, deepening their kiss.

Zach spared a fleeting thought for the partygoers inside the ballroom, who if they happened to glance outside would see him and the woman he loved making out while their baby was nestled between them, safe and sound and loved. He just couldn't muster the energy to care, every piece of him committed to loving this wonderful woman.

'Zach,' Phoebe mumbled against his lips, pulling abruptly back from his kiss. 'The baby's moving. It happened for the first time this morning. Quick.'

She grabbed his hand and held it to her stomach, her eyes alive with excitement and love.

Zach held his breath, certain that nothing could

make this moment, their declarations of love, any more perfect. And then it happened, the faintest tap against his palm.

'Did you feel it?' she asked, her eyes wide with wonder.

Zach nodded, almost overcome with love, ready to fall to his knees and kiss the life their love had created. 'It's magical. You're magical. Everything I'll ever want.'

They kissed again, only breaking apart when the wolf whistles and cheering began from the open doors of the ballroom, where a small group of the wedding party had gathered, including the bride and groom and Phoebe's friend Ali.

Phoebe laughed, covering her mouth with her hand. 'Ignore them,' she said, tugging his waist and resting her head over his heart with a contented sigh.

'Come on, she said, looking up at him, 'I want to introduce my man to my crew.'

Zach smiled and slipped off his jacket, draping it over her bare shoulders in case she was cold.

'Lead the way,' he said, taking her hand and following her inside to where the party raged until dawn and the rest of their lives began.

EPILOGUE

Seven months later...

PRESSING A KISS to Zach's cheek, Phoebe swished the skirt of her bridal gown—an elegant ivory sheath with embroidery around the bust and following the edges of the low back—aside and left her new husband's side, already missing the way his hand rested between her bare shoulder blades every time they stood close.

Heading for the table where her three best friends were gathered, she waved over at the Wilson family—Emma, Aaron and the healthy nearly one-year-old twins, Poppy and Jasmine—and then cast one more glance over at her darling boy, Noah Henry Archer, who was being thoroughly spoiled by all three of his grandparents. Smiling as Noah reached for her mother's elegantly perched fascinator, causing Rosa, Henry and Veronica to laugh, Phoebe sighed contentedly.

'Your speech just now made me cry,' said Ivy

as Phoebe joined them at their table, dabbing at her red eyes with a balled-up tissue. 'It's a beautiful wedding.'

Phoebe hugged each of her three maids of honour in turn, lingering to show them how much she valued both their friendship and their support. She would never have made it through the first three months of motherhood without her friends or without Zach. It turned out that everybody needed a crew, and together with her sexy husband, and Noah's incredible grandparents, these three amazing women were it for Phoebe.

'I told you the pregnancy hormones were a killer.' Phoebe laughed, winking at Ivy as she slid into a spare chair at the table. 'But at least you and Lucas get to enjoy the other…shall we say *side effects*?'

As a collective giggle erupted, a waiter appeared with a tray of fresh champagne glasses. Phoebe and Ali helped themselves to bubbles, both Harper and Ivy declining by raising their flutes full of water.

'She's not wrong.' Harper winked suggestively, one hand rested on her six-month baby bump. 'It's been four months since our wedding, but Yarran and I are still very much in the honeymoon phase, if you know what I mean.'

'We know what you mean,' Ali said, rolling her eyes. 'But please, for the love of your friend, do *not* elaborate on the details of my brother's sex life.'

All four women laughed as Harper slung an arm around Ali's shoulders and pressed a smooch to her cheek, leaving behind a perfect kiss of red lipstick.

'A toast to Phoebe and her gorgeous boys,' Ali said, raising her glass, her stare a little misty.

'Cheers!' The others joined in and they all took a drink.

'I too have a toast,' said Phoebe, once more holding her glass aloft. 'I didn't know when we were medical students that you three wonderful women would be the most important friendships of my life, but here we are.' Her throat closed up as she glanced at her friends, meeting their stares in turn.

'I won't be here for long,' heckled Ali playfully, rescuing Phoebe from ruining her mascara with tears.

'I meant metaphorically, but yes, Ali, we all know that you and Jake are off on another adventure overseas. Just remember to send us a postcard from your world travels.'

Phoebe smiled as Ali glanced over at Jake, who was out on the manicured lawn with Yarran and Lucas, all three of them tossing around a rugby ball with Yarran and Harper's son, Jarrah.

'But what I really wanted to say,' said Phoebe,

sobering, 'is that you three have been there for me through my pregnancy and with the wedding and with Noah, in ways I could never have imagined when we were all younger. So thank you. To you, my darling friends. I am so happy that we have travelled together to this point in our lives, friends for ever. To Ali and Ivy and Harper.'

They clinked glasses, both Harper and Ivy welling up once more.

'I can't take any more hormonal tears,' Ali said, laughing as she stood. 'I'm going to cuddle Noah in case crying at the drop of a hat is contagious.'

Phoebe blew her a kiss. 'Don't try and steal him. I'm watching you,' she called after a retreating Ali.

Just then, Zach motioned her to join him once more.

'Excuse me, ladies, but my new husband needs me,' Phoebe said, ignoring Harper's lewd comments and Ivy's dreamy stare as she made her way back to Zach's side, her overriding thought how much she needed him in return.

'I missed you,' he said, pressing a kiss to her lips, his hand once more finding her bare back.

'I missed you, too,' she said, smoothing the lapels of his tux jacket. Her heart hurt at how gorgeous he looked. She couldn't wait for the wedding to be over so they could be alone.

'It's time for our first dance as husband and wife,' he said, taking her hand and leading her to the dance floor, signalling to the band to play their song.

'I'm so happy,' Phoebe said as she glided around in his arms, her feet barely touching the floor. 'Thank you for our beautiful boy.'

They looked over to where Zach's dad, Henry, was holding the baby up to watch his parents' first dance, his chubby little arms and legs jerking excitedly.

'Thank you for being mine,' Zach said, tilting up her chin so he could whisper a kiss full of promise over her lips, uncaring that all their friends and family were watching.

'Always,' she said, getting lost in his stare.

'I'll hold you to that promise, Mrs Archer,' he said, and swirled her around and around.

* * * * *